HOME IS WHERE THE HORROR IS

C.V. HUNT

Published by Grindhouse Press
PO BOX 293161
Dayton, Ohio 45429

Home Is Where the Horror Is
Grindhouse Press # 033
ISBN-10: 1-941918-20-4
ISBN-13: 978-1-941918-20-3

Other Titles by C.V. Hunt

Fate

Up against your will

Through the thick and thin

He will wait until

You give yourself to him

-Echo & The Bunnymen, "The Killing Moon"

For Andy

Do you think the last five years would've been any different
if I would've picked Texas Roadhouse instead?

1

The edge of the woman's buttock was blurred. I ran my finger over the touchpad of the laptop and zoomed in on the photograph. I inspected the sharpness of the large diagonal scar starting on the woman's back a few inches from her spine and slightly above her waistline. The scar snaked across her back, crossed around her waist, and plummeted into the dip where her hip and lower stomach met before tapering to an end. The scar was crisp in the photo but I'd forced the focus of the camera on the imperfection and it caused the other areas around the tissue to blur. It made the viewer focus on the scar alone and it would lead one to believe the scar was the main focal point and the only reason for the photograph. But I wanted people to see the picture as a whole. I wanted them to see the contrast of the surrounding flawless skin severed by the enormous scar. The model's small breasts were in shadow, as was her face, to keep the subject a non-sexual distraction. But the unfocused part of her buttock bothered me the most. I flipped to the next photo I'd taken in the set.

The model's pose and the lighting were exactly the same as the previous photo. I hadn't forced the focus in the shot. I'd managed to capture the scar and the unmarred skin in complete clarity in this photograph. I scrolled over the photo slowly, looking for imperfections needing touched up. I couldn't find any. Her pose was perfect. The lighting was perfect. The contrast of the ugly scar against the flawless skin was perfect. There were no distortions in the photo. Her face and breasts fell neatly into the shadows of the picture. I fought the urge to screw with the lighting and contrast in the program because I knew I would spend hours and hours making minuscule adjustments only to become frustrated and revert to the original photograph and realize it looked better than anything I'd done to it.

I moved the edge of the photo to crop a large portion of the woman's head and legs out of the frame. The picture became a disembodied torso. Some viewers would wonder what the woman's face looked like. They would want to know what her expression was. Did she feel sad about her disfigurement? Was it an accident? Was it a lifesaving procedure and was she proud to have survived it? Some of those answers could be read in the person's face but I always choose to leave that aspect of the photograph out unless the scar or malformation was on the person's head or the model's expression brought something unique to the subject. Then the harrowed or happy expression was left in the photograph and played with the mood of the person viewing it. Most people would focus on the contrast of the scar when there was no face to determine how they should feel about the particular piece. And there were a handful that would see what I saw.

I repositioned the photo slightly within the cropped section. This would become the final photo.

No one would know her face. But I knew. And the model knew. It would be up to her whether she wanted to reveal her identity and how she felt about the scar when and if I chose to exhibit or sell the photograph. I labeled the photograph appropriately and saved it to my computer. I would order a physical print and frame once I was done with the set. I scrolled to another photo from the shoot.

A light rap on the door behind me gave me a start and broke my concentration. The clock on the bottom corner of my computer displayed 10:03 P.M. I assumed it would've been closer to eleven. Eleven was Naomi's bedtime and she always informed me when she was turning in for the night. I had gotten up early to take the photographs I was currently looking at and was excited to edit them. I didn't know why she was knocking on my door an hour early other than to have a conversation with me or inform me she was turning in an hour early. And we'd had the conversation numerous times before about bothering me while I was editing photos. Unless it was urgent I didn't want to be interrupted once I was in a certain mindset. I assumed she was informing me she was turning in early then and didn't bother to stop what I was doing.

The photo on the screen in front of me was a slight variation of the previous photo I'd cropped and saved. I didn't care for the angle and deleted it immediately. It was replaced with a photo of the woman from behind. The emphasis was on one half of her buttocks and the part of the scar on her back.

The knock sounded again, louder this time, and the door opened. I kept my focus on the photo on the screen. It was standard for her to knock, crack the door, give a quick good night, and retreat to the bedroom.

"Evan?" Naomi whispered.

"Yeah," I responded. I actively suppressed my aggravation of the interruption.

I zoomed in on the photograph and the puckered part of the scar on the woman's back filled the computer screen. I squinted at the image and added a filter to soften the lighting.

She cleared her throat. "Um . . . can we . . . ?" She trailed off before rephrasing. "We need to talk."

The four most destructive words known to mankind flew from her mouth and drilled through my back to strike my heart like lightning. My hand froze on the keyboard. In a split second I knew this was it and I let the reality and inevitability of what was about to happen sink in. I stared at the scar on the screen, took a slow deep breath, and swallowed. Somehow the moisture in my mouth had managed to completely disappear in the couple of seconds that had passed. My Adam's apple caught when I swallowed and I suppressed the urge to cough.

I knew something like this was coming. I had mentally prepared myself for this even though I'd told myself it was all in my head. The longer it went on the more I'd convinced myself I was blowing things out of proportion and overthinking the situation. But I knew this was the finality of the tiny insect bite that happened to our relationship after Naomi's birthday. It was like the smallest mosquito bite that itches and burns and you scratch and scratch until it's raw and you choose to ignore the festering sore you've dug until it's transformed into something more insidious and it's too late to dab a little hydrocortisone cream on it and nip it in the bud. Now you have an abscess. Now you have gangrene. Sorry, sir, now we have to amputate for the greater good.

A part of me hoped she was going to bitch at me for not helping out around the house as much as she'd like. I could handle that. We'd had that argument off and on for years and I'd learned to tune out the persistent drone of her nagging when she decided it was time to beat that dead horse every six months. For once in our relationship I hoped she wanted to spend an hour complaining about how my photographs and the two days I worked at the coffee shop down the street weren't making enough money and I should give up what I loved and find a full-time job to help out with expenses. I'd dealt with that scenario at least a dozen times and managed to convey what the photography meant to me and avoided having to find a mindless nine to five job, or God help me, resort to working in a fucking factory. Maybe she wanted to strike up a conversation and work in some passive aggressive jabs while informing me of how one of her friends was getting married, or having a baby, or buying a house in the country, like I gave a shit about any of her condescending friends. But I knew better. And my suspicions were completely fed and validated with the small phrase that always strikes the fear of life changing speedbumps into anyone's heart that hears it: We need to talk. This had been a long time coming. It had been like sitting around waiting for a bomb to tick down to zero but having no idea how much time was left. There was no blazing and oversized clock. Just an overwhelming sense of doom. I could hear it in her voice when she'd uttered the sentence: We need to talk. She'd spoken the words with a resolution that punctuated the end to a frustrating and dissatisfying story where the protagonist's world crashed down around him while his friends are handed everything they could ever ask for. And the silence between the two of us at this very second was like the animals growing quiet right before a major disaster strikes.

Naomi had infected our relationship with her unrest a few months prior. She began working longer hours. She hung out with her friends more frequently. She stayed out longer. She was hardly ever home other than to eat, sleep, or shower. And her sex drive plummeted drastically. I would've been an idiot not to know something was amiss. Sure, I had worried about what might have been happening. But I was at a loss as to what to do to fix it and if I had to be truthful with myself I wasn't sure I wanted to fix it. My paranoia amped into high gear once our sex life slowed down to an unenthusiastic performance once every two weeks. I tried harder to please her in bed. I spent more time on foreplay. But all of my attempts were met with sighs of aggravation and a disinterest in anything other than for me to hurry up and finish, which made me feel like an inadequate asshole to the point where I grew disinterested in having sex with her. It made me question my ability to be a good and attentive lover. Jerking off made me feel less guilty and was more satisfying.

It started shortly before her thirty-fifth birthday. I had

equated it to an early mid-life crisis. She'd always wanted things I didn't want and voiced them off and on throughout our relationship. But the urgency in her arguments began to hit a level I could only describe as desperate. She attributed my inability to resign to her wishes to me being five years younger than her. I wasn't ready for what she wanted and I didn't know if I ever would be. Deep down I knew my stubbornness to change was stronger than my desire to stay with her. And I kept hoping she would bend to what I wanted eventually. I knew I had commitment issues and it had a lot to do with my upbringing. But there wasn't anything I could do to fix that without thousands of dollars being poured into therapy I couldn't afford, and in all honesty, didn't want. I also didn't want to work at a job I hated. I didn't want to get married. I didn't want to have kids. And I didn't want to buy a house. I was content with the way things were. Stability kept me content. Once I established a life I was comfortable with it was nearly impossible for me to flip it on its head. And Naomi wanted a different life.

I knew when she'd expressed her desire for those things it would only be a matter of time before we had this conversation. I didn't have to see her face to reaffirm this was the end of the line. She was ready for *the* 'we need to talk' conversation. And honestly, I was surprised it had taken her this long to come to terms with her inner conflict. She was smart. She was strong. She didn't need me. She knew what she wanted. And I would never provide her with what she wanted. Time was running out for her. Thirty-five was the halfway point between responsible adult and getting too old to keep dragging your feet. Each day that passed brought her closer and closer to the latter.

Dread seeped into my soul and I suppressed the urge to let it poison my attitude. This had to be done. Begging her to stay or dragging it out would only make it worse for the both of us. My throat was tight and I tried to swallow again but my throat was so parched. I shoved my emotions into the void deep within me, a place I'd learned at an early age was a great dumping ground for anything that made me appear weak, and I regained my composure. I tried to work my tongue on the roof of my mouth to produce some saliva.

"Evan? Did you hear me?"

I spun my chair around to face her. She'd removed her make-up for the night and her bobbed hair hung damp around her face. I couldn't recall hearing the shower run but I had been too engrossed with the photographs to be aware of anything happening in the townhouse. The skin under her eyes was puffy and red as if she'd been crying. She looked exhausted and wore an expression of terror mixed with sadness. The word 'haunted' came to mind as I stared at her face. She stood in the doorway and appeared reluctant to enter my claustrophobic office overflowing with oversized framed photographs and shipping supplies. Her eyes darted to a three by four foot black frame holding a close up I'd taken of the cellulite on the back of an obese model's thigh. She observed a couple of the other photos—a woman's chest with double mastectomy scars and another of the residual limb of an amputee. She clenched her hands into fists and rubbed her thumbs together in what I'd grown accustomed to know as a nervous gesture.

"What is it?" I said.

"Um." She thumbed over her shoulder. "Can we talk in the

living room? The photos are ... distracting." She tucked a strand of damp hair behind her ear.

"Okay."

I could hear the fake inflection of my voice. It was a mixed falsehood of cheeriness and perplexity. I was neither happy nor confused but I didn't want to make this any harder for either of us. I felt like I was about to deliver my greatest acting performance aside from the time when I was eleven and lied to Mom about who started a small trash fire in the alley behind our house, blaming it on some neighborhood kids.

I stood and motioned for her to lead the way. It was only a few steps from any one room in the downstairs of our townhouse to another. She led me to the sofa and sat on the edge as if she didn't want to get too comfortable. My stomach sank and hurdled through space and time and defied the laws of gravity as it bounced and hurt and made me nauseated. It was the same feeling I got when I rode a rollercoaster. The sensation seemed appropriate for what I was about to go through. I was a born pessimist. Or maybe I was a made pessimist once my father was gone. But up to this moment I still had a miniscule amount of hope we weren't going to have *the* talk. The talk of all talks. The talk that would put us both out of our misery. Well, it would put her out of her misery. I was quite content with my life and my surroundings if I could only subtract Naomi's growing iciness toward me and the lack of satisfying sex. I could tell by her body language the next few minutes were going to be the end of my current situation and I suppressed the anxiety of having to move and upend everything I'd grown accustomed to.

All of this was ending: the townhouse, the furniture, the

dishes, the towels, the television, the food in the kitchen, the ugly green rug by the door. It was all hers now. She'd purchased all of it. She made everything the way she wanted it. Except me. I was the one plate with a chip on the edge from where it was dropped while washing or the towel that unraveled a little more each time it was washed. These things were still functioning and useable but they were a thorn in the side every time you looked at them and thought, *I should throw that out and replace it.* She was hell-bent on exchanging the comfort of the relationship. Excuse me, sir, this one didn't live up to what it promised. Is it still under warranty? I'd like to exchange it. I was about to be dropped in the defective bin and inspected for a factory refurbish, if salvageable.

I took a seat beside her and mirrored her posture, sitting on the edge of the seat. I understood why she wanted to do this in the living room. We wouldn't be facing one another. She didn't have to look at me when she told me. She rubbed her thighs as if her palms were sweaty and stared at the coffee table with a million mile expression peppered with concern.

She said, "I don't know where to start. This is so hard."

She rubbed her palms on her thighs harder and lifted and tightened her shoulders in a tense gesture. I let her fidget for a few seconds, waiting for her to go on. I decided the best option was to pull the drain plug for her, break the seal, and let the rest come tumbling out.

I said, "Does he treat you good?"

The question caught her off guard. It caught me off guard too. It wasn't how I wanted the conversation to go but it was the question at the back of my mind all these months. Who was she fucking? Was he better than me? Did he have a bigger dick? Did he fuck better than me? Did he have more money? More friends? A nice car? A house? Did he own expensive suits and have a job with his own office and his name on the door? Did he go to the gym five times a week to work on his six-pack? Undoubtedly so. My intent wasn't to make her feel guilty though. At least I didn't think I wanted her to feel guilty. I just wanted her to come clean. I wanted her to admit it and stop making me feel like an asshole because our relationship was falling apart. Yes, I was one of the reasons everything had gone south. But she chose to put more and more distance between us and drive a stake to separate the us. The stake had a name but I didn't know who he was and I didn't want to know. I didn't want to meet the man she deemed better than me. But I guess there was a small smug part of me that wanted to rub her nose in what she'd done wrong. I wanted her to know she wasn't as clever as she thought she was. She was a trope. And I wasn't stupid or ignorant. I knew she had been up to something and this was coming. I also chose not to intervene because the work I would have to invest to put things back together didn't seem worth it. The work wasn't worth the reward to me. If you could call it a reward. What would I gain? Me being paranoid and jealous and secretly letting what she'd done and apologized for eat at me every day and every moment she wasn't in the same room as me. That didn't feel like much of a prize to fight for.

She flinched at my halfhearted accusation and looked at me with an astonished expression. She blinked rapidly and began to appear frightened before stuttering something unintelligible in answer.

I thought I wouldn't be bothered to know she was sleeping with someone else. Because I already knew deep down what was happening without being told. But her expression said it all. She wasn't a good liar. I felt as though she'd punched me in the gut as she sputtered and tried to come up with an excuse or lie. It wasn't the confirmation of the allegation that hurt. It was the fact she was going to deny it even though I could see it was true.

I gestured for her to stop. "Don't," I said. "Please don't lie to me. You at least owe me that much. The lie hurts more than the betrayal."

Her eyes rimmed with tears. She turned her gaze back to the coffee table, rubbed her thighs again, and nodded. She whispered, "I'm sorry." Tears slid quickly down her cheeks and dropped onto her pajama bottoms. She wiped her face with the back of her hand.

"It's not your fault. It's my fault. This has to be done and you'll feel a lot better once you get it out. So just say it."

I would take the blame for this because if I would've given her what she wanted she wouldn't have had to find a replacement for me.

She turned to me and another tear rolled down her cheek. "Aren't you mad?"

I hated to see her cry. I wasn't a sadist. It wasn't that I didn't care about her and that was the reason I'd rolled over and let it all happen. I wanted to see her happy and I wasn't willing to be something I wasn't to give her what she wanted. Yes, I was upset she was having sex with another man. But it made her happy. And once this was over with it would all tumble into place for her: the wedding, the kid, the house. There wouldn't be any more chipped plates and unraveling towels. It would all be fresh and clean and new for her and everything she ever wanted and hopefully she'd be able to cling to that happiness and ride it out till death. We'd been together for seven years. I knew her well. She had Christian-like morals when it came to relationships and the secret coupling was eating her alive. I was raised by a single mother and instilled with the idea that an independent and liberated woman was one you supported, not condemned, even if her ideals didn't exactly conform to your own. If this was what she wanted I wasn't going to stand in her way any more than I already had.

"Why should I be mad?" I said. "As long as you're being honest with me. If you'd been fucking him for a while and I happened to find out instead of you telling me I'd be mad."

She flinched when I said the word 'fucking'. She rubbed her hands on her thighs again. I laid my hand on top of hers to stop her from fidgeting.

"Stop acting nervous," I said. "It's making *me* nervous."

"You're too calm," she said. "I keep expecting you to freak out and start screaming."

"Have I ever screamed at you?"

"No."

"Why would you think I would do it now?"

"Because I'm a horrible person. Because I just told you I'm having an affair."

It was my turn to flinch. We stared at one another silently, waiting for the other to make the next move. The word 'affair' had fallen from her mouth effortlessly but its impact was shattering and final. To me the word affair was far more of a damaging word than fucking. Affair implied an emotional connection with the person you were cheating with. I let go of her hand and sat back. Naomi stared intently at the floor as if she were ashamed to look at me. I stared at her back as she shifted away from me. The movement was miniscule but it made me cringe. It was as if she were readying herself for the onslaught of an attack. If she shrank away from me much more she would be cowering. I had to put a stop to this. I couldn't handle watching her beat herself up over something I was partially responsible for.

I said, "The brutal truth is I'm not going to fight to keep you."

She lifted her hand to her mouth to stifle a sob as if what I'd said was the equivalent to a slap in the face. Her shoulders jerked as she cried into her hand. I was thankful I couldn't see her expression. I was being insensitive on purpose. If she was going to use a man to drive a wedge between us I was going to use hurtful words as an axe to sever us completely and put our relationship out of its misery. I didn't want there to be any chance of reconciliation. If we were going our separate ways and in a few months she realized she'd made a mistake and toyed with the idea of eating crow I wanted her to think back to the hurtful things I'd said now and reconsider bothering me for a second round of dissatisfaction. Because I knew I would relent if she asked me to come back, and living in a relationship where I knew without a doubt I was a placeholder would destroy what self-confidence I had.

"I can't give you what you want," I said. "It would make me

unhappy if I did. You've found someone who wants the same things as you. I'm not going to beg and plead for you to stay."

She wiped her eyes with the back of her hand and took a deep breath. I waited for her to acknowledge me. She continued to avoid looking at me.

I said, "I couldn't live with myself knowing the only reason we're together is because I begged you to stay . . . knowing you'd rather be with someone else. If you stayed I would lose respect for you for not standing up for yourself. And I can't trust you anymore."

She took a shuddering breath and sniffed.

I said, "If we stayed together after this I would drive myself insane. I would constantly worry you were cheating on me . . . because you'd done it before."

She spun toward me. Her face was blotchy from crying. "I would never—"

I cut her off. "I'm not saying you would. I'm saying I would forgive you. I'd never mention it again. But every time you were an hour late, or called to say you had to stay late at work, or made last minute plans with your friends . . . there would be a small monster in the back of my brain reminding me you'd had an affair once before." I almost choked on the word affair. "And I forgave you. And if I forgave you once it would be nothing for me to forgive you again . . . and again . . . and again."

She nodded to convey she understood. She finally sat back on the sofa. It wasn't a gesture of relaxation or even one of defeat. She collapsed into the cushion from exhaustion. We both stared at the black screen of the television for a moment.

I broke the silence. "And I'm not going to beg for other obvious reasons."

She spoke without taking her eyes off the television screen. Her words were monotone and emotionless, as if she didn't care what else I had to say. "What's that?"

"I don't want to get married. I don't want to have kids. And I'm sure as fuck never giving up photography." I waited a beat for her to respond and when she didn't I added, "I don't think you could live with yourself if all of a sudden I was willing to do those things anyway. I know I wouldn't be able to live with myself if I bullied you into doing whatever *I* wanted. Controlling each other's dreams turns you into a parent. I don't want to live with my mother."

She acted as though she were going to say something but caught herself. I was sure it was a retort to the mother reference. But she'd thought better than to bring up the subject of my deceased mother and I silently thanked her for it. It had been a year and a half since Mom passed and for the most part I was over it. But every now and then there was the pang of loss when talking about her or reminiscing of my childhood. Naomi tiptoed around the subject of parents after my mom's death. She knew I was protective of my mother and anything that could be construed as negative against her. Naomi's parents were both still alive and together. She didn't have the first clue of what it was to be an orphan other than observing the situation through me and my brother.

I said, "I'll sleep on the sofa tonight."

"You don't have to move out right away," she said. "You can sleep in the bed." She hesitantly said, "I can stay . . . somewhere else. You can stay here until—"

"No. No." I cut her off. "I'll be gone tomorrow. I don't want to be here any longer than I need to be. I have to leave. I don't want to be cuckolded. Being here would make the situation a constant forethought. If we're going our separate ways I'd rather make a clean break. Besides, there's nothing tying us together but the address. I'll call Phillip. I'm sure the two of us can have my stuff cleared out by the time you get home from work tomorrow."

"I can give you some money—"

"I don't want your fucking money."

The sentence was delivered gruffer than I'd intended. But it was true. I didn't want to be indebted to her in any way.

"I'll stay with Phillip until I find something." I suppressed a passive aggressive jab about my income because I knew it would turn into a fight about how I should've gotten a real job. "You know how to get ahold of me if you need anything."

She nodded. "So that's it?"

"Guess so."

"It feels like a weight has been lifted. I mean . . . I feel better but it feels weird between us now."

"How's that?"

"I don't know. Now that the sexual aspect of our relationship is completely off the table it's weird. Because . . . I still care about you. I want you to be safe and happy. It sorta feels like we're really good friends now."

I wanted to tell her there was no way in a million fucking years I ever wanted to be her friend but I pushed it into the void with the devastated emotions threatening to spill over. And I didn't want to be that guy. The guy who wishes evil and vile misfortunes on their ex because they felt they were wronged. The venomous feeling was there but I was actively choosing to ignore and suppress it. Naomi wasn't a bad person. She was a selfish person and only doing what was right for her. Tomorrow I would move in with my brother and his wife and kid. I would wait a short time for the call or email or visit where Naomi told me she'd made a mistake and I would force myself to be strong and tell her not to bother me anymore because I didn't want to be reminded of what she'd done and I didn't want her to settle for second best. But I didn't expect for it to happen. I was sure once I stepped out the front door for the final time it would be the last time I would ever talk to her. Seven years of my life gone. Just like that. And I wasn't going to sit around and stew in self-pity over the whole ordeal. I was moving on. It was my own pettiness and selfishness that wanted her to eat crow. And even if it did fail for her it wouldn't change anything. I would never step foot in this place again. She needed to find what she wanted and stop trying to mold me into something I didn't want to be. This was over.

"Yeah," I said, "I know what you mean." I patted her on the leg. "You okay?"

She nodded and rubbed her thumbs together again.

I stood. "I'll sleep on the sofa tonight." I took a couple of steps toward my office.

"Where are you going?"

I stopped. "I was in the middle of working on a set."

She opened her mouth to say something but I ignored her and made my way to the office. There was no need to rehash the situation. There was no need to reminisce. There was no need for us to continue talking to one another.

I entered my office and shut the door in time to clasp a hand over my mouth. I suppressed the sob welling in my chest before Naomi could hear it. I'd be damned if I let her know how wrecked I was over the whole thing. I cleared my throat and took a deep breath to compose myself. This wasn't the end of the world and crying over it was only a self-pitying act. Tomorrow was the beginning of something new.

2

Phillip entered the garage holding the last box from the trunk of his car. "Any special spot for this one?" He hefted the box awkwardly to keep from dropping it.

"I guess with the rest of them," I said. "Nothing important." I pointed to the small pile of garbage bags and boxes we'd dumped on the floor of the garage away from the path of cars.

"Are you taking any of this inside?" He carefully placed the box with the others.

I meticulously rearranged the framed photos and stacked them against the wall of the garage. The last thing I wanted was for Phillip's wife, Holly, to hit them when she pulled into her parking spot. I knew she wasn't happy about me moving in and didn't want to give her another reason to hate me.

Scrutinizing one of my photos I said, "I'll grab my clothes and bathroom things. I don't need the other stuff around me all the time and I don't want to clutter up your house." I thought,

Holly doesn't want me to clutter up the house.

Holly and I didn't care for one another. Never had. She probably saw *me* as clutter. She made it clear the first time I met her she didn't like me for whatever bizarre reason because I had never been anything but courteous to her from the first minute we met even though after five minutes I thought she was a bossy know-it-all bitch. She was controlling and—even though she'd never admit it—got knocked up on purpose so Phillip would drop out of college and get a shitty job at a call center and marry her and be forced to give her all the attention she needed. And she needed *a lot* of attention. Phillip doted on her after he dropped out of school so *she* could get her degree. I always wondered why he stayed with her when her main hobbies included making Phillip miserable and encouraging their twelve-year-old daughter to be a snotty brat. But I knew he would never leave her unless she told him to leave. It was the same reason I waited until Naomi decided it was time for me to concede from the relationship. When your father choses to take *the* final exit without any warning it fills you with a sense of abandonment as a child and you cling to anyone who'll pretend to love you for as long as you can and you'll do anything to make the relationship appear fulfilling for the other person. Phillip and I had spent our adult lives trying to make up for our father's suicide. We carried the burden of pretending everything was okay on the surface level to break the cycle of emotional trauma and not let it manifest in other destructive ways.

Phillip stared at the pile of boxes we'd built while I anxiously nit-picked the placement of the frames. I wasn't used to seeing him unkempt and in ratty clothing. He wore a paint-stained T-shirt with a large rip in the armpit and his jeans were on their way to disintegration. It also appeared he had skipped shaving this morning. Phillip's job had a dress code and required him to wear a button down shirt and dress pants. And for the most part he continued to wear his work clothes on his days off. I assumed Holly would berate him endlessly if he happened to stain one of his good shirts and this was the reason for his homeless attire today.

He looked over the pile of my stuff and said, "You don't own much." He shifted his weight from one foot to the other and rested his hands on his hips.

I left the photos and joined him. I pulled two of the garbage sacks full of clothes from the pile and tossed them toward the door leading to his kitchen. "There should be a shoe box with my bathroom stuff." I found the box and retrieved my laptop bag and said, "Don't think I can live without this. You sure this stuff isn't in the way?" I double checked the proximity of my belongings to the path of an incoming car from the overhead door. I gingerly set the laptop and bathroom supplies on the ground by the bags of clothing.

Phillip eyed the prints leaning against the wall of the garage and approached them. He said, "They're fine."

I'd rested the frames with the photos facing out. His gaze stopped on a photo of a woman's small naked breast and midriff. The prominent focus of the print was on the well-formed supernumerary nipple a few inches below her breast.

He scratched below his ear nervously and said, "Can we flip the photos around?"

I stared at him for a second, wondering why he wanted the

photographs turned. I said, "I guess so." I approached the photo he was scrutinizing and flipped it to face the wall. I said what I was thinking. "Shame on you, breast."

Phillip made an aggravated noise. "There's nothing wrong with the photos. You know I like them. It's just—"

I interrupted him. "Holly hates them."

"Yeah. Sorry. This sucks. I mean . . . not you moving in—"

I spoke in a nobleman's ancient, "Out with it, man." I mimed slapping him in the face with an imaginary glove.

He spoke slowly as if searching for the least hurtful selection of words. "Holly has expressed her concern about how long you'll be staying and . . . what kind of influence you'll be on Makayla."

I blinked and tried to process the absurdity of his statement. "What kind of influence *would* I be on Makayla? She's twelve. I don't think I can damage a pre-teen girl. I'm sure she's wrapped up in her own microcosm of problems and peer pressure. Besides, you know me. I'll be in my room ninety-nine percent of the time working on the computer. No offense to you and your . . ." I rolled my hand to insinuate his house, "thing you have going on here. Believe me, I don't want to stay here any more than she wants me here. I can only kiss someone's ass who hates me for so long."

"There's two more weeks before school lets out for summer vacation."

"I would think Holly would be happy to have a free babysitter. I'm only gone a couple of days a week to work at the café. I'm sure I could talk to the manager and move those days to the weekend so I don't spoil your family time."

"Makayla won't be happy. We promised . . . Holly promised to let her stay home alone this summer without a sitter. It's time she started learning to take care of herself."

"At twelve?"

"She's mature enough."

"All the more reason not to let her stay home alone. Do you remember being twelve? What we wanted to do to twelve-year-old girls?" I waved my hand dismissively. "Forget I said anything. It's none of my business. Teach her how to shoot a gun and be into right wing politics. What do I care? It's not my kid."

"Makayla has changed a lot since you last saw her at Christmas. She's gotten into some dark shit. Holly's worried she might take an unhealthy interest in your photos."

I nodded. "Yeah yeah yeah. Okay. I get it. It's not the girl who has issues. It's me living in the house causing her preexisting issues. Whatever makes wifey happy. I forgot. I'm the goddamn devil." I held my pointer fingers to my forehead, opened my mouth, and flipped my tongue back and forth. I growled, "I'm the fucking devil!" I ran up to him and pretended to hump his leg while growling, "Give me your virgin women so I can corrupt them and fuck them and sacrifice them for the greater good!"

He pushed me away. "Get away from me, psycho! Are you ever going to grow up?"

"No need to," I said and went back to flipping photos around. "You know I'm only here long enough to save some cash and get a place of my own. Two months tops. And I'm not going to interfere with whatever form of methodical brainwashing you two have scheduled for Makayla. If I wanted to control another human being I would've gotten a dog or had a kid myself. And I definitely had the opportunity." I waved my hand around to insinuate my surroundings. "It's the reason I'm standing in your dank ass garage having this conversation."

"Naomi wants kids?"

"Among other things."

"What things?"

"For me to get a steady job. To get married. A bunch of shit I don't want." I flipped another photo and avoided looking at him. Thinking about Naomi made my throat and chest feel tight. I knew my emotions would be readable on my face and I didn't want Phillip to notice. "Look, I don't want to talk about it unless you're a certified psychologist. Taking advice from someone who's never dealt with the same situation probably isn't a good idea."

"Okay. We won't talk about it."

He stepped forward to help me flip the remaining frames. When we were finished he lifted the two garbage bags of clothing by the door and I carefully retrieved my computer and bathroom effects.

We entered the kitchen and I was assaulted by an air freshener I didn't like. The smell stung my sinuses and had a high floral note similar to cat urine. I sniffed and resisted the urge to sneeze. His kitchen was vast with a large stone top island in the middle that doubled as a table. I'd been to their house for holidays and knew the formal dining table was in a separate room but only used for special occasions. The kitchen was open to the living room, creating a great room with high ceilings.

We crossed the kitchen and entered the living room area. I noticed their wide-eyed Siamese cat, Pete, standing by the sectional. He raised his hackles once he spotted me, hissed, and ran off down the hallway, disappearing into the last bedroom on the right.

"Ignore him," Phillip said. "He hates everyone except Holly. He'll tolerate me if I'm feeding him but that's about it." He led me down the hall toward the bedrooms. With his hands full he tilted his head toward the first open door on the left and said, "Makayla's room."

He entered the room directly across from Makayla's. I remembered Makayla's room from five years ago when Phillip and Holly first purchased the house. They'd painted it a hideous shade of pink at the girl's request and filled it with white furniture overflowing with girl things: dolls, clothes, stuffed animals. There was nothing particularly interesting or original about her room and no desire to pay any attention to it any time after seeing it once. I always stopped in briefly for the holidays with Naomi and I couldn't ever recall looking in the girl's room any other time when passing it to use the restroom. Phillip's house was designated as the gathering place for family events because it was spacious and he had an extra bedroom for Mom to stay overnight. Mom had lived three hours away. And a three-hour drive one-way was if the weather was good. Which could be a crapshoot during the winter holidays. And Mom always looked for any excuse to stay a couple of days and spoil her only grandchild by taking her to the mall and buying her whatever she wanted.

I peeked into Makayla's room and found it had drastically

changed from the last time I remembered seeing it. The walls were now painted flat black and covered with posters of bands wearing corpse paint. There was a poster of Anton LaVey above the head of her bed. A large statue of Baphomet sat on a vanity I once knew to be white but had been painted black, poorly. The number 666 was carved into its tabletop. Bottles of black nail polish and make-up paraphernalia were scattered across the vanity and the border of the mirror housed magazine photos of groups of men dressed in black morbid costumes with makeup darkened eyes and long black hair. There was a small section of the mirror exposed in the center which was smudged with fingerprints and had a sloppy pentagram drawn on its surface with what I assumed was black permanent marker.

Phillip emerged from the room across the hall. "Told you she's changed."

"I'd say. I guess the devil has already done his job. I don't know what kind of terrible influence Holly thinks I'll have on the kid."

He pointed to the bathroom door down from Makayla's. "You'll be sharing a bathroom with her."

I took a few steps down the hall and inspected the bathroom. It was the same plain, cramped bathroom I'd remembered using a few times before. But now black eyeshadow cases, eyeliners, and lipsticks were scattered across the white countertop, along with black stains of either makeup or hair color dotted around the sink.

"Sorry about the mess," he said. "I'll make her clean it up."

"Don't worry about it." I pushed some of the makeup stuff out of the way and set the shoebox with my toothpaste, toothbrush, deodorant, electric clippers, and other odds and ends on the counter. I briefly worried about Dad's old-fashioned razor and the loose razorblades in the box but assumed if the girl had violent tendencies Phillip would've warned me.

"You'll have to fight her for it in the morning until school is out. She spends an hour and a half in there getting ready in the morning. You could use ours if—"

"I don't think it'll be a problem. I take my showers in the evening. I only brush my teeth, take a leak, and put on some deodorant in the morning."

"She sleeps twelve to fourteen hours a day on the weekends. So I don't think it'll be much of a problem once school is over."

I carried my computer to my temporary new room. Phillip followed me. The walls were lavender and the color made me cringe. The queen-size bed and white dresser didn't leave much space to move around. There was approximately three feet of space surrounding the bed and a tiny closet in the corner. Phillip had set the garbage bags full of clothes on the floor by the bed, which was covered in a floral pattern duvet. I sat my computer on the bed.

"Sorry about the décor," he said. "It was decorated for Mom."

An awkward moment of silence passed between us. I knew we were both thinking about her but neither of us wanted to bring her up. The hurt and sorrow and raw emotional state of the wound caused by Mom's death had healed the best something of that magnitude could. But the scar tissue was translucent and tender and the slightest prodding could cause the wound to burst open and drown both of us.

I tried to lighten the mood. "It's better than sleeping in my car. I don't have a lot of options right now."

Phillip rubbed the back of his neck nervously. "Do you need any help putting things away?"

We both avoided looking at the other.

"I think I'm good," I said.

"Well, I'll let you alone. The girls will be home in a couple of hours. Figured we'd order pizza tonight."

"Sounds good."

"If you need anything . . ."

He left the statement hanging. He was insinuating he was open to talk but I didn't think either of us was equipped to deal with the unrestrained emotions. He shifted his weight from one foot to the other and fidgeted before crossing his arms over his chest. I could sense he was worried I was about to break down bawling and pour my problems on him. And I wasn't completely sure if he was implying we should talk about Mom or Naomi. He took my silence as a pass on his offer.

He said, "I'm gonna watch some TV."

I nodded. "Okay."

He crept out of the room and closed the door gently behind him. And I was left to make myself as comfortable as possible in a house where I wasn't wanted and in a room decorated for a dead woman.

3

Holly brought home two pizzas, along with a sulky Makayla. We situated ourselves at the island in the kitchen. Holly and Phillip sat beside one another on one side of the island while Makayla and I sat across from them.

Holly and Phillip's postures were polar opposites. Phillip slumped and I recognized his demeanor from our childhood. A brooding Phillip as a child was no different than a brooding Phillip as an adult. Holly sat ramrod straight. Everything about Holly was stiff and impeccable and always had been. Her blond hair was sleek and shiny and smoothed into an intricate bun. I used to assume the fancy bun hairstyle she wore took several hours to achieve but I was sure by this point she had perfected it over time and now it only took her a couple of minutes in the morning. She had an air of efficiency and perfection that always left me to wonder if she'd been raised in a military family. I couldn't remember a time she'd worn her hair any other way, starting a year after her and Phillip were married. And as usual, her makeup looked freshly applied and her pantsuit was wrinkleless. I imagined while the rest of the world slept in beds Holly either submerged herself in a vat of formaldehyde or slept in a coffin. She was always pressed and flawless and wore the expression of a cold marble statue. While the rest of us ate with our hands, Holly used a knife and fork to keep her well-manicured hands clean. She'd cut a small piece, lift each bite daintily, and slide the food from her fork with her teeth to keep from disturbing her lipstick. I'd always had the strong urge to shove her down into a mud puddle.

Makayla didn't appear to care as much about her makeup which struck me as strange since she wore three times as much as her mother. Her eyebrows were shaved and she either couldn't be bothered to draw new ones on or didn't know how. Her eyes were heavily rimmed with smeared black eyeliner and eye shadow and her lips were painted black and in need of a fresh application. Her lipstick had worn in such a way that it looked as if it was actually the remnants of some dark hard candy she'd consumed. Her white foundation was possibly composed of several layers to cover the massive amount of acne she was obviously self-conscious of and was still easily detectable even with the numerous coats she'd spackled it with. She hadn't bothered blending the makeup beyond her jawline and there was an obvious contrast between her face and the skin of her neck. All of Makayla's clothing was oversized and black and fought to hide the fact she'd gained a few pounds since the last time I'd seen her. To top off her new makeover she'd colored her long blond hair black. And all of her hair, with the exception of her too short bangs, were wadded and knotted into dreadlocks. She slumped sideways in her chair, her elbow on the counter to keep her in a semi-upright position, and her face inches from her plate. Without her elbow supporting her non-contributing mass and exhausted looking frame I was sure she would slide from her chair and pool on the floor. She pulled pepperoni from her pizza and nibbled on it with fingernails painted with severely chipped black polish. She gave me a look I could only read as disgusted as she ate.

No one spoke and I couldn't shake the feeling the three of them were miserable. It wasn't so much a feeling but a giant painting on display. All you had to do was look at them. They appeared as if my presence was the driving reason for this forced family interaction and it was painfully apparent none of them so much as spoke a word to each other on a daily basis let alone sit at a table with each other for more than two minutes. The complete silence, aside from the sounds of us eating, was disturbing. I was used to the sounds of traffic and pedestrians passing on the street at all times of the day and night. I was accustomed to the sounds of the city and they'd become comforting to me. The quiet of the suburbs was eerie and the whole situation made me feel extremely awkward and unwanted.

I took it upon myself to break the silence. "So . . . Makayla, what grade are you in now?"

The girl stopped picking at her food and gave me the most appalled look, as if I'd shat on the island in the middle of dinner. The girl turned her head, still supported by her hand, to her mother with a questioning gaze, as if to ask if it were okay to ignore her intrusive uncle. Holly turned her attention to her daughter for a beat. A silent conversation slipped between the two of them before Holly turned to me and answered for her daughter.

"She's in seventh grade," Holly said. She turned her attention back to her plate and stabbed a miniscule piece of pizza she'd cut from her slice.

I reflected on myself in seventh grade while everyone continued to eat in silence. I remembered the sense of confidence I had when I was that age. The recognition my body was changing and maturing and within a few short years I would be a man. I also remembered masturbating like a fiend whenever there was the slightest opportunity to be alone for five minutes and stealing the ten-year-old porno magazines Phillip had acquired from a schoolmate whose father would never miss the magazines from his extensive collection. I bit my tongue to keep from reminiscing about my sleazy pre-teen years to Phillip there on the spot and had to suppress a chuckle.

I addressed Makayla. "I took an afterschool photography class in seventh grade. They taught me how to develop thirty-five millimeter film . . . back before everything went digital." I nodded toward Phillip. "Your dad took a woodworking class in high school."

Phillip started when I spoke his name. He was completely enveloped in his own reverie or thoughts or misery or some imaginary land that wasn't here with his stuck up wife and snotty daughter. He simply said, "Yeah," and straightened slightly in his seat. He mumbled, "A lot of good it did me." He took another bite of his food.

I wanted to slap myself in the forehead for sticking my foot in my mouth. I refrained from automatically saying 'I forgot the bitch made you get rid of most of your tools because you spent too much of your free time doing something you loved and not sitting around with your family to stare awkwardly at each other and wonder why the fuck you were being forced into a social interaction with the people who despised you the most.'

I asked the girl, "Do you have any extracurricular activities?"

Makayla's expression hadn't shifted from her initial reaction to me. She continued to observe me with disdain, slumped in her chair. In a disgusted tone she said, "How long are you gonna be here?"

Phillip spoke around a bite of food. "Makayla." He said her name with a reprimanding tone, warning her.

She snapped, "What?"

Holly said, "Don't be rude." She leaned forward and smacked the top of her daughter's hand picking at the pepperoni. "Stop playing with your food."

"I'm not hungry . . . *Mother*." She said the last word venomously.

I redirected my conversation to Phillip and changed the subject. "How's Mom's house going?"

Holly shook her head and made a disgusted sound. It was obvious the subject of Mom's house was one they'd argued about several times and she hadn't quite gotten what she wanted. Or she was tired of arguing about it.

Phillip appeared shocked anyone was trying to have a casual dinner conversation with him. He said, "It's not going. I don't have the time to put into it right now. The drive. The work. I can only get to it on the weekends." He side-glanced in Holly's direction and paused as if waiting for her to retaliate against something he'd said before continuing. "I work all week and hate spending my free time doing physical labor instead of spending it with my family." His upper lip on the right hand side twitched the tiniest bit the way it always did when he lied.

My brain screamed, *Liar!* He didn't want to be near his family and it was excruciatingly apparent. But his acidic family wasn't the only reason he wasn't working on Mom's cabin. He was a sentimentalist. And I knew he would drag his feet when he took on the project because he didn't want to sell the place even though it wasn't our childhood home. The home I considered our childhood home was the house our parents lived in when Phillip and I were born. It was also the house our father committed suicide in when I was seven and Phillip was ten. The house our mother abandoned shortly after. When I was in my early twenties I used to drive by it occasionally. I never stopped, only slowed down as I passed to see if anything had changed. The house always appeared to shrink each time I saw it and I almost didn't recognize it once when the current occupants at the time had taken it upon themselves to cover the worn white paint with a fresh coat of sky blue. The house wasn't located in the greatest part of the city and, eventually, the owners either gave up on it or fell upon hard times. It was abandoned and quickly fell into disrepair and became a target of vandalism. I drove by once and someone had spray-painted a noose on the front door. A few months later someone had broken out several of the windows. It was then that I realized the house had most likely become the root of haunted urban legends for the local kids due to Dad's actions. I imagined it became a place for teenagers to hide and smoke pot or drink a few warm beers they'd pilfered from their parents' refrigerators or for a few lucky bastards to pester their underage girlfriends into losing their virginity on some random stained mattress left behind by a previous tenant. I imagined the inside was worn and battered and littered in cigarette butts and cigarette burns and beer bottles and cans, the place reeking of urine and stale come. A year after the broken windows appeared I drove by and the house was gone. As if it never existed. As if the lives and love and holidays and memories and tragedy that took place under its roof never existed or weren't important enough to preserve. The house had been demolished.

Calling anything home after leaving that house when I was a kid was a joke. It always felt by the time we settled into a new place we were on the move again. We never lived in one place for more than a year or two. Mom was always looking for 'a safer place to live' or 'somewhere with a better school system' but as I grew into a teen I recognized these as fibs. Mom lied or explained her way out of the endless phone calls from bill collectors and numerous yellow envelopes that arrived in the mail with the large red word 'overdue' stamped on the front. The 'safer place' and 'better schools' were something she told us instead of admitting she'd been let go from another job and we were being evicted again. She jumped from job to job. Sometimes she worked two or three jobs to keep food on the table. Sometimes when she was let go from a job she locked herself in the bathroom and cried for an hour. All it took was for one of us to get sick, or for her to get sick, or for the car to break down and the finely tuned budget of supporting our family was thrown into chaos. She finally got a break after Phillip and I moved out. She found a decent job at a high paying factory and began to save her money. And eventually she had enough to purchase the cabin and her retirement kicked in. The cabin was on the edge of a state park and was one of two on a secluded dead end road. Both structures were originally used as rentals for couples or small families who vacationed in the area. The owner split the property and sold them after falling ill and not being able to manage them any longer. I'd never been to the cabin but Mom brought pictures along during holidays shortly after she'd purchased it. She was so proud of the place but I was sure she was just happy she'd managed to finally find some security in owning a home.

Holly snapped, "Just sell it." Her gaze flicked to me and she softened her next statement. "Both of you wouldn't have to worry about it anymore and you could split the profit."

It was noticeable they'd had this argument a hundred times. And you'd have to be ignorant not to be blatantly aware Holly was purely interested in the money. It was written all over her. From the top of her meticulously salon colored head to the tips of her expensive pedicure. My bringing up the subject struck a nerve with her. Hell, my existence struck a nerve with her because it meant once the cabin sold she would only get half the money.

Phillip sounded irritated. "We've gone over this. If we do the repairs we can sell it for more."

She rocked her head from side to side, inviting the image of a snotty teen girl, while she stared at her plate and cut another piece of her pizza. "And in the meantime it's costing us money to pay the property taxes and utilities."

Phillip inhaled deeply and let it out slowly. He took another bite of his pizza and ignored her to insinuate he was done arguing. Phillip's method of arguing was to state his piece calmly and immediately shut down so the argument became one-sided and couldn't continue without the other person looking like a raving lunatic. Nothing much about him had changed since childhood. I knew he didn't want to talk about it anymore with Holly and I couldn't blame him. She wanted him to sell it. He wanted to sate her money hungry ways. And I wasn't sure if he was working on it so he could get a chance to do something he enjoyed every once in a while or because in doing so he was able to escape being around his family for a day. I didn't want to put Phillip in an awkward position of fighting with his wife but I was genuinely curious about its progress. As much as I'd love to see Holly squirm for the money, and for the remodeling to be prolonged, I could have really used some cash in my current predicament also. And the more the better.

My photography kept the utilities paid when Naomi and I were together and my two days a week at the coffee shop afforded me to put gas in my car, pay for upkeep on said car, and buy a book or two or an album or go see a movie now and then. Even if the cabin wasn't sold for much it was better than nothing and unless I took up working at the coffee shop full-time I didn't see myself being able to afford a place of my own for a long time. The money from Mom's cabin would keep me afloat for a while if I kept to a stingy lifestyle and it would give me time to figure out how to make more money from my photography. Maybe I could become a wedding photographer.

I asked, "What's left to be done to the cabin?"

"We've already spent the money on the supplies," Holly said. "It's just sitting there collecting dust." It became clear she wasn't speaking to me but trying to continue her and Phillip's argument. "You could list it and add the cost of the materials to the asking price. All the buyer would have to do is hire someone to do the work . . . or do it themselves."

Phillip ignored her and answered my question. "The wood floor still needs to be refinished. That little dog she had did a number on the finish. The bathroom is done but the kitchen still needs to be gutted. The cabinets and countertops are sitting in the storage under the cabin. She had those awful particle board cabinets and I bought real wood replacements."

I asked, "Whatever happened to Mom's dog?"

"My Pete hated that dog," Holly said indignantly. "We put it up for adoption at a no-kill shelter. None of my friends wanted to take in an animal that wasn't completely housebroken."

I thought, *No.* You *didn't want to take in a dog that wasn't completely housebroken.* I couldn't imagine the type of person who chose to be friends with Holly. I decided she probably didn't have any friends at all and referred to her coworkers as friends because aside from Phillip and Makayla and her hairstylist and manicurist they were the only people she saw on a regular basis. Those coworkers would most likely be mortified to find out the office ice queen told people they were her friends.

Makayla pulled the layer of melted cheese she'd picked free of toppings off her pizza. She lifted the congealed blob above her head and ate it as if she were a royal subject being fed grapes. Once she'd stuffed it all in her mouth she noisily sucked the grease from her fingers.

Her mother reprimanded her. "That's not ladylike. Stop playing with your food."

"I'm eating it, aren't I?"

Holly gave her a stern look, turned her attention back to her own plate, and changed the subject. "Do you have homework?"

"Does it matter?"

The two exchanged defiant expressions yet again in silence.

"I could help you," I told Phillip. "Actually . . ." A thought struck me. "Let me throw this at ya. What if I moved out there and worked for free in exchange for rent? Once the work is done I'll find another place and you can sell it. You won't have to drive out there all the time and I'll take care of the utilities and taxes as long as I live there."

Makayla and Holly dropped their impending battle and turned their attention to me. I recognized an expression of approval immediately on Phillip's face. He turned to Holly for the final answer. I could see the wheels of dubiousness turning in her head. It was hard to decipher Makayla's thoughts on the situation through her heavy makeup and lack of eyebrows—of which the latter factored into a person's ability to exhibit facial expressions naturally—but she appeared expectant and marginally excited herself. Of course the girl wanted me out of the house. She wanted the place to herself throughout her summer vacation to do whatever it was she wanted to do . . . sacrifice a goat . . . host a satanic teen orgy.

Holly made an uncertain sound and cleared her throat.

"A year," I said. "I won't be there more than one year."

"I think it's a good idea," Makayla said.

I could tell from the silent exchange passing between Phillip and Holly this was something they wanted to discuss without me in the room. Or without Makayla whining about how she'd been promised to have a solitary run of the house. And it was also obvious nothing was ever executed or approved in this household without Holly's full consent.

I said, "Maybe I should let you guys discuss this."

Phillip turned his attention back to me. "We'll talk it over."

I nodded. I tried to finish my pizza but found my appetite had disappeared. I was celebrating inside because I knew Holly wanted me in her home about as much as she wanted a bedbug infestation. I wanted to celebrate. I knew the cat was in the bag and I would have a place to myself soon. My hunger was replaced with a craving for a beer. I would have to go out later and make a stop at a bar to have a couple celebratory drinks. I couldn't buy a six pack because Holly approved of alcohol about as much as she approved of anything or anyone else in her life.

4

Phillip's car crawled down the narrow, curvy two-lane highway. I trailed him in my own car. Overgrown trees and brush lined the highway and I knew he was having difficulty finding the road to the cabin. My GPS had stopped working five miles back and I was sure his was in the same state. I couldn't remember the last time I went anywhere without relying on GPS to get to my destination. I was panicked and lost without the guidance of the small digital blue triangle hovering above the road on the screen of my phone and the calm female voice notifying me of my approaching turns and telling me when to merge. Phillip warned me about the poor cell reception and told me I would probably want to purchase a physical map of the area if I needed to get around until I memorized the roads and landmarks. The state park wasn't a complete dead zone for cellphone signals but damn close. I eyed the screen of my phone again, hoping it had picked up a faint signal, but no luck.

I checked my rearview mirror to make sure a line of cars hadn't formed behind our slow moving caravan. The sharp curves, combined with the dense flora, had me paranoid a car would come speeding around a corner any moment and rear end me before the driver could realize I was doing half the speed limit. The road was an accident waiting to happen if you didn't at least keep up with the posted speed. Currently there weren't any cars behinds me. I turned my attention back to Phillip's car.

A movement on the side of the road caught my attention. A wild turkey scuttled into the thick brush, followed by three baby turkeys. Their sudden appearance excited me as I observed the last little bird trip on some long grass before bouncing up and disappearing into the thicket.

Phillip's passenger side turn signal began to blink and his brake lights illuminated. I spotted a lone pole with two green signs extending horizontally from the top containing house numbers. Beside the pole were two mail boxes and the entrance to a narrow and steep driveway. A blue dumpster was situated across the road, opposite of the drive. I made a mental note of the landmarks. I would have to rely on them and my odometer to get around until I found a map.

Phillip eased his car onto the steep drive and proceeded cautiously. I gave him a wide berth before turning onto the drive and following him.

Once all four of my tires were situated on the abrupt slope the framed photos in the back seat flipped forward and clacked loudly against each other when they hit the back of my seat. I cursed under my breath and hoped the jostling hadn't caused any damage to them. The pitch of the drive, combined with the fact it was graveled, made the descent terrifying. I couldn't imagine driving up or down the drive with the slightest amount of snow or rain, especially in my ancient Honda with balding tires. It felt as if the gravel would give at any second and my car would slide down the slope, crash into Phillip's pristine new car, and the both of us would fly into the dry ravine at the bottom.

Phillip reached a sharp ninety degree turn and the road leveled beyond that point. My car whined as I held the brake and turned onto the horizontal path. Just beyond the edge of the gravel drive was a sharp drop on the driver's side. The roof of Mom's cabin could be seen a couple hundred feet ahead. The top of the cabin was a few feet above the level of the drive with the foundation set into the slope of the ravine. A set of wooden railings on that side of the drive were the only indicator for the steps that descended to the cabin. Someone had gouged out parking spaces in the inclined earth across from the steps. The parking area was barely enough room for two cars.

Phillip parked and I pulled in beside him. There wasn't a lot of room in between our vehicles. I slipped out of my car cautiously, holding my door tight, terrified it would bang into Phillip's car and scratch it. I knew he wouldn't be upset about a scratch but I was certain he would never hear the end of it from Holly. Phillip had less trouble exiting his vehicle.

Phillip said, "I guess we should unload the trunks first, huh?"

"Not a lot of room for parking," I responded.

"You plan on having large dinner parties?"

"If anyone ever came to visit they'd have to move in. I don't know if they could make it back up the drive."

Phillip walked to the trunk of his car and opened it. "You

saw the mailbox and dumpster, right?"

I mimicked him and opened my own trunk. "Yeah."

"Mom always complained about having to climb the drive to take out the trash and check the mail. I think she drove her car up to do it." He stacked a box on top of another in his trunk and lifted them. He nodded over his shoulder. "She ended up having the neighbor do it when she got sick."

I peered down the drive and Phillip's gaze followed mine. Approximately one hundred feet farther down the drive the road ended in front of another cabin. The structure was built more level with the drive and was located on the opposite side. The place was cast in dark shadow by the massive trees surrounding it. The darkness made the place appear ominous. The other cabin sat on short stilts instead of having a concrete foundation like most houses, leaving the crawlspace open to the elements. A battered maroon station wagon was parked in their parking spot, fashioned similar to mine.

A woman in a white cotton dress stood on the heavily shadow-covered porch, watching us. She had long brown hair and appeared pale and thin. It was hard to discern much about her from the distance. A gruff male voice sounded from somewhere and the woman hastily retreated into her cabin. Her exit was punctuated by the hard slap of wood from the spring-hinged screen door.

I said, "They seem friendly."

He shrugged and started toward the steps. I grabbed a few things and followed him.

The steps were wooden and fashioned into two tiers. A small landing separated the tiers. The steps ended at an elaborate deck running along the side and back of the cabin in an L-shape. Once we reached the door at the side of the cabin I noticed another set of stairs descending to the ground at the back of the cabin.

I took in the heavy foliage and severe angle of the ground. The ground was mainly covered in decaying leaves and pine needles. There wasn't much in the way of grass due to the massive trees shading the majority of the ground and restricting the sunlight. Phillip set down his boxes and fumbled with the keys.

I said, "I guess I won't have to worry about mowing?"

He opened the door. "Nope. The only yard tool she owned was an axe to cut away fallen branches and to chop wood for heat." He retrieved his boxes and entered the cabin.

I'd forgotten the cabin didn't have a conventional heating system. Mom had told us how much of a pain it was to set an alarm in the middle of the night so she could throw a couple of pieces of wood on the fire to keep it from going out in the winter.

When I entered the cabin I was hit with the overwhelming stench of sawdust, dust, wet dog, and the dry heat of an attic. The weather of the last two weeks had been mild. Summer was threatening to happen any moment. But the cabin was a tad too warm and I attributed it to the place being shut up and the sun beating down on the metal roof.

The layout of the interior was one giant room with the exception of the restroom having been walled off with a sliding wooden door installed. The kitchen was located inside the door we'd entered and ran all the way across and up against the wall separating it from the restroom. The rest of the cabin had no distinguishing features except for the ordinary fireplace situated catty-corner from the restroom. The ceiling was high and the wood beams were exposed. Two ceiling fans with lights were suspended from the main beam running along the peak of the roof. The walls were the exposed timbers of the wood constructing the cabin. With the absence of furniture the wood floors appeared scarred from the nails of Mom's dog.

Phillip set his boxes on the counter. He said, "I would've never gotten rid of her stuff if I'd thought you'd need it."

"It's okay. That's what credit cards are for."

We both chuckled.

He pulled his cellphone from his pocket to check the time. "When did you say the cable guy was arriving?"

"Between two and six."

"We better get my car unloaded so he has a place to park."

I nodded and crossed the cabin to the backdoor which opened onto the sizeable covered deck surrounded by railing. The view overlooked a thick mass of enormous trees. I left the door open and proceeded to open the four windows and turn on the two ceiling fans to air out the place. When I was done I helped Phillip to empty his car of my possessions. Luckily I hadn't bothered unpacking much in the two weeks I'd inhabited Mom's old guest room and it took us less than an hour to reload everything back into both of our cars.

Once we'd emptied his trunk he backed his car out of the parking space so we could fully open the rest of his doors and retrieve the remaining items. He returned his car to its original spot when it was completely unloaded and we proceeded to do the same with my car.

At one point during the many trips up and down the stairs I turned my attention to the other cabin. I couldn't be completely sure but thought I could make out the outline of a figure standing inside the screen door. It didn't appear to be the woman from before, but a tall and broad-shouldered man. Whoever it was took a step backward and disappeared into the shadows of the cabin once they became aware I was watching them.

When the cars were empty there was an hour to spare before the earliest scheduled arrival time for the cable installer. Phillip led me down the flight of stairs ending at the ground behind the cabin. Where the cabin on the path had an exposed crawlspace this structure was on much taller stilts and had a much bigger space underneath because of the severe slope of the ground. Someone had taken advantage of the space opportunity and enclosed the area with corrugated sheets of metal and transformed it into a small garage. There was a standard door and a narrow overhead garage door on the side facing the back of the cabin. Phillip unlocked the man-size door, pulled a string a few steps in the door to turn on the light, and showed me the breaker box, the water heater, and the washer and dryer hidden behind the mountain of cabinets, countertops, buckets of stain and varnish for the floors, and a myriad of screws and fasteners and hand tools to perform the work needing done.

"You'll have to rent a floor sander to do the floors," he said. "But everything else is here. And the cabinets too. It's just a matter of doing it."

"Well, I don't have a lot going on right now. No girlfriend. No job other than the photography. I might have to make a few trips to the post office. I'm sure I'll have plenty of time to work on it."

He went on to tell me if I made a right at the end of the drive there was an all-purpose convenience store, greasy spoon, and gas station combo a couple miles down the road. It was an overpriced tourist trap for the visitors who came to roam the state park and hiking trails. He instructed me to continue down the road for another twenty-five minutes and I would run into a small city home to a twenty-four hour one-stop mega store and a couple of hardware stores. He briefly contemplated staying until the cable guy came and went and driving with me so I wouldn't get lost and he could help me haul my groceries back from the store. I reminded him of my landmark memory and told him I'd be fine and needed to learn the lay of the land myself since I was going to be living here for a while and he should head back home and try to beat the rush hour traffic. He reluctantly agreed.

I got the feeling Phillip didn't want to go back to his family. There was an envious vibe from him that surprised me when he handed me the hokey skeleton key for front and back doors of the cabin along with a small battered brass key for the garage door. I wasn't sure if he was jealous because *I* was going to do the rest of the work to the cabin—the type of thing he loved to do—or if he wanted to be in my shoes. No partner telling me what I could and couldn't do and demanding I give them all my attention and still not being satisfied when all their demands were met. No ungrateful kid who didn't give a shit if I lived or died as long as I continued to hand them an allowance so they could buy things I didn't approve of. No brainless nine to five job, the only thing remotely interesting about it being the paycheck. Did he want what I had? Did he really want the crippling loneliness and solitude and poverty that was my new existence? Because once he was gone and I was faced with the silence of being alone in the middle of the woods I began to question whether it was what I really wanted.

5

The cable installer didn't arrive until six o'clock and I was starving by then. I hadn't thought to bring a snack and Phillip had thoroughly cleaned the refrigerator and cabinets once Mom was gone. It wouldn't have done me any good had there been food. I didn't have any dishes or pans to cook or eat with. I resorted to chugging water straight from the kitchen faucet to stave off hunger pangs. While waiting for the installer I occupied myself by walking around the outside, phone in hand, and searching for a signal. I found the reception was finicky and there was no rhyme or reason to where or when the reception would work or not and most times it didn't work in the same spot twice. I found if I stood on the deck near the stairs descending to the ground beneath the cabin I could pick up one bar of signal. Once I had a faint signal I tried searching for some basic furniture I could afford online. There were a couple of sites for stores nearby but once I clicked on the link my phone responded by informing me there was no signal. My cell-phone was a couple of years old and I wasn't sure if it was the reason my Internet and cell reception were so poor or if all phones would have the exact same problem.

When the installer arrived he acted put out and complained about how difficult it was to find the place. He was an over-weight man who sweated profusely and acted like it took a great effort to descend the stairs with his tools. He repeatedly tested my patience by trying to upsell me with introductory offers for the first fifteen minutes after his arrival before he even began the work. I was starving and becoming more irritable the long-er he hemmed and hawed before getting to work. Apparently it was unheard of to only want Internet and no television or phone package. The man was pushy and overly authoritative and condescending for someone whose career wasn't extremely desirable and didn't require extensive educational requirements. It took several denials and repeatedly telling him I only wanted an Internet connection before he made a passive aggressive jab about spotty cellphone reception and how I'd regret it. I briefly pondered if I should relent and allow him to at least add a land-line but I didn't have a lot of money and I was cranky and hungry and damned if I was going to let him gloat in his suc-cess of bullying me into spending more money. I wasn't sure if he worked on commission or not and I didn't care. I was broke and I wanted him to hurry up before I died of starvation. It was only after he was satisfied he'd gotten the last word in that he finally got to work.

My stomach grumbled loudly while the man fumbled with the installation and I almost literally ran out of the cabin once he was gone. My stomach was hollow and after repeatedly filling it with water I was certain it had decided to consume itself along with some other vital organs to keep me alive. My thoughts were so focused on food I nearly forgot my wallet in the process of leaving.

My car whined as it climbed the drive and I made a right-hand turn like Phillip had instructed. I made a mental note of my odometer and the landmarks as I drove and found the lone convenience store with a hand painted sign identifying it as The Pit Stop. There was no way a person could miss the place. It had an overflowing parking lot, gas pumps, and an abundance of half-occupied picnic tables under a worn canopy. There was nothing else in the area except for a few scattered houses here and there along the road, punctuated with signs to caves, waterfalls, and hiking trails.

The store was a nightmare. It was full of trinkets and shirts and all the garbage a family would want to buy as memorabilia when on vacation. There was a small sad section in the middle of the store with a few last minute canned items, condiments, potato chips, soda, and a freezer full of pizza and ice cream. They also had an extremely limited selection of overpriced beer. The register area was packed with people buying beef jerky and potato chips and soda and the counters were stuffed with cigarettes and lottery tickets. I found a restaurant on the opposite side of the store from where I entered. But the extent of their menu was whether you wanted ketchup or mayonnaise with your fries and you could only order a medium pre-topped pizza with your choice of cheese, pepperoni, or supreme and there was no place to sit and eat inside. The eating area was at the picnic tables outside regardless of the weather. There were myriad signs throughout the place informing the customers the store had hidden surveillance cameras and shoplifters would be prosecuted. The store's clientele didn't deviate much from a certain type of people I'd actively avoided my entire life. Their clothes and manner of speaking were trashy, something I associated with people I would've called rednecks. There were only a few exceptions. There was a couple dressed in cycling apparel who acted as horrified as I was at the spectacle. It didn't dawn on me until later that camping was a poor family's idea of a vacation. The workers appeared hostile and unwilling to help any customer. They would huff and condescendingly answer people who asked them if the store carried a particular item or where they could find something specific. I resorted to grabbing a random bag of chips and a bottle of water and paying three times the normal price for them before returning to my car. I ate the chips hastily as I drove to the town Phillip told me I would find if I continued down the road. I told myself I would not shop at that store ever again unless it was absolutely necessary and I wondered if Mom had shopped there.

The town was less frantic. I stopped at the first fast food joint I spotted and ate three dollar burgers before moving on to the mega one-stop store.

I didn't normally shop at megastores. I assumed the larger store would be as thriving and overfilled with the type of people I'd encountered at The Pit Stop. But the place was surprisingly quiet and docile. I made my way through the store and filled my basket with the cheapest bare essentials for the kitchen, bathroom towels, bedding, cleaning supplies, and some basic first-aid things. I ended up with two stuffed shopping carts. I paid for the items and unloaded them all into the car before reentering the store to purchase groceries. I made sure to stock up on beer.

By the time I returned home it was nearly dark and I was exhausted. I unloaded the car and put the food in its proper place but piled the nonfood items in the middle of the floor. I drank a beer and stared at the mountain of stuff I'd purchased and tried to suppress the panic attack of how I was going to pay for the growing debt I was compiling on my credit card. The alcohol calmed me and I told myself there was no harm in making the minimum payment for the rest of my life. I also reminded myself I needed to change my ads for models to reflect my new location and tried not to fill my head with negative thoughts about how I would never receive another inquiry from someone willing to be photographed because I was out in the middle of nowhere and people would think it was some elaborate plot to lure them into the woods and murder them. My worries rolled from one thing to another: no one around here appeared to be remotely interested in the arts let alone be interested in modeling nude if need be, I needed to make more money, I needed to substitute my income with a another part-time job if I couldn't make enough from my photography, where would I find a job, what if I got sick and died and no one found me for three months because I didn't have a phone to call an ambulance, and lastly, was Naomi happier now? I put it all out of my mind and proceeded to construct a makeshift bed on the floor out of the bedding I'd purchased. I couldn't remember the last time I'd slept on a floor—most likely when I was a child—and knew I wasn't going to feel great in the morning, if I was able to sleep at all. I thought of scouring the Internet and trying to find furniture but I was too exhausted. I would make furniture hunting a priority tomorrow.

I forwent establishing an Internet connection or checking email messages. I'd received a text while shopping from Phillip informing me he made it home safely. I responded in kind when I had a strong reception signal at the store. I didn't need to know much more. The world was just me now and the only other person I was remotely worried about was Phillip. I checked my phone but there wasn't a signal and the battery was almost dead.

I downed another beer to help me sleep. I left the windows open since the weather was perfect and I was still combating the dog smell. I turned the lights off and the cabin was plunged into complete darkness. I told myself I should purchase a night-light until I got used to my surroundings. I used the light of my phone to find the pile of blankets and pillows I'd constructed. I made myself as comfortable as I could under the circumstances. The silence of the woods was unnerving. I was used to the clamor of the city and I found it difficult to fall asleep even after a couple of beers. Time was hard to measure without the city sounds and I contemplated getting up and having a couple more beers. I eventually fell asleep after focusing on the faint rhythm of insects.

A sound woke me in the middle of the night. It took me a few seconds to realize it was coming from outside. It sounded as if something were being dragged across the ground for a second, followed by a pause, and repeated again. Scrape. Silence. Repeat. Whatever it was it sounded large and my sleep-fogged mind struggled to put an image to it. It wasn't the sound of a raccoon dragging a piece of trash. The sound conjured images of a large animal dragging oversized prey off to its cave. The image of a bear dragging a fallen tree branch to wherever it was constructing its home came to mind. It went on for a few minutes, fading a little each time. Eventually I couldn't hear it anymore and drifted off again. Right before I dozed off I wondered if there were Yeti in the area

6

In the morning I was woke by the rhythmic rapping of a woodpecker. My back was stiff and my thighs ached from the exertion of repeatedly climbing the stairs the day before. I did some slow and deliberate stretching while I was still on the floor. My muscles protested and the ache of them being stretched was equal parts pain and pleasure. Relieving my painfully full bladder fell into the same category. When I was done in the restroom I dug through my plunder from the previous day and opened the coffee maker and bean grinder.

Once the coffee was brewing I retrieved a pan, cooking utensils, and the dishes I would need to eat. I washed and dried them with a hand towel that left lint on everything it touched. I cursed aloud as I tried to rid the dishes of the lint and resorted to drying the dishes with a paper towel. I prepared a quick breakfast and once I was done eating I proceeded to open the rest of the items in the pile, wash all the kitchen equipment, and store them in their respective places.

I constructed a pile of the towels to wash, reminding myself to buy a laundry basket on my next trip to the store, and collected the trash. All of the boxes and their internal packaging amounted to three large trash bags. I decided I might as well take the bags to the dumpster before I got absorbed in searching for furniture online.

The bags were light and I was able to manage all three at once. My thighs protested when I started up the stairs. I thought, *I should have taken a couple of Tylenol when I woke up.* At the top of the stairs I looked for any sign of movement from the other cabin. I didn't spot anyone or hear anything coming from that direction.

I made the trek up the drive on foot and deposited the bags in the dumpster across the street. On my way back I checked the mail box and found a stack of junk mail addressed to Mom.

As I walked down the drive a wind picked up and the trees began to sway and rustle noisily. A shadow passed over the drive and a rumble of thunder sounded in the distance. I looked up to see a darkened cloud traveling quickly to blot out the sun. I picked up my pace.

Mom always complained how quick the weather would change in the area. She'd joked about how the weatherman would forecast a sunny day with no chance of rain in the morning and by the evening it was pouring buckets. I remembered the phrase she used to repeat was 'Mother Nature was a loose cannon'.

A few drops of rain landed on the stairs as I hurried down the steps to the cabin. I was winded when I reached the door. I wasn't used to running and my legs felt like overstretched rubber bands from the previous day's activities. I thought I might want to start some type of exercise regimen sooner or later. I wasn't exactly overweight but I also wasn't an Adonis and the thought of possibly finding another woman who might be remotely interested in having sex with me made me self-conscious of my lazy and untoned thirty-year-old physique.

I flung open the screen door and stepped inside the cabin. I stopped short and my heart jumped into my throat when I realized someone was in my cabin. An old man stood in the living area with his arms crossed, observing the pile of towels on the floor with a scowl. He looked up at me, scowl still intact, when I entered. His eyes were a pale shade of blue and his gaze was intense. He was thin and sinewy and tall with a full head of white hair. The way he stood made it apparent he was ablebodied but the thin skin and deep wrinkles of his face told a different story. He appeared to have dealt with rough times from the wear of expression. I was unsure how to interpret his age.

I didn't know what to do. I'd never dealt with a home invasion before and thought the likelihood for such an event would've been more statistically plausible when I lived in the city. Even though the man looked older than me I was aware he was completely capable of doing me physical harm, not to mention I didn't know if he possessed a weapon. I wasn't sure if I was getting robbed or what the situation was I'd stumbled into. The man didn't make a move to introduce himself or apologize for the intrusion or explain why he let himself into my house. In fact there was an element of defiance to his posture and facial expression as he continued to stare at me.

I suppressed the urge to raise my hands and tell him to take whatever he wanted. I decided to act strong and ignorant to any wrongdoing on his part. I hoped if he was planning on robbing me my appearance was unexpected and my ignorance would give him a chance to invent a story for his presence and he could apologize and leave without a physical altercation.

I managed to sound firm. "Can I help you?"

He said, "You the new tenant?"

I expected his voice to be feeble but it was firm and confident. I could tell by the slight movements he made that if I was being robbed it wasn't going to end well on my part.

"Yes," I said. "This was my mother's house. I've inherited it for a short time."

He gave a half smile that made him appear cruel before he became expressionless once again. Large drops of rain pelted the roof. I suppressed a shiver attempting to run down my spine. I was filled with a sensation of fear and goosebumps rose on my forearms and back. There was something off about the man. The words that came to mind were 'inhuman' and 'wrong'. I wanted him out of my house in the quickest fashion possible.

He must have sensed my apprehension. He unfolded his arms and put his hands in his pockets and tried to appear more casual. He wore short sleeves and when he unfolded his arms I noticed two thick scars running down his inner forearms, from wrist to elbow. Two more words invaded and echoed in my mind: suicide scars. I averted my gaze and wasn't sure if he'd caught my recognition of the scars.

He said, "I'm your neighbor. Name's Lloyd."

"Oh," I said. I closed the gap between us and extended my

hand. "I'm Evan."

He stared at my hand and it was clear he was not going to shake it. I glimpsed at the scars on his forearms again and had an overwhelming desire to photograph them. But Lloyd didn't strike me as the type of person who'd understand or appreciate what I was trying to accomplish by photographing his scars. In fact, a tremor of panic surged through me as I realized he may have already pawed through my things while I was gone, discovered my photographs, and this was the reason for his cold demeanor. I dropped my hand awkwardly, took a step back, and side-glanced the photos stacked against the wall. Phillip had stacked them picture side in and I silently thanked him.

Being closer to the man did nothing to dull the ill feelings in my gut. The only sound was the patter of rain now steadily falling and a faint rumble of thunder.

"Uh." I struggled with how to respond. "Would you like something to drink? Coffee? Water? Beer? That's about all I have at the moment."

"No, thank you. I saw people fooling around down here again. I wanted to make sure squatters or thieves weren't ransacking the place."

"No, sir."

His eyes narrowed as if my response had offended him. "Your momma was a nice lady. Kept to herself."

"No worries here," I said. "I'm a private person myself. You and your wife won't hear a peep from me."

"Daughter," he said. He clenched his jaw.

I couldn't put my finger on the reason for his aggressive and dislikeable attitude. It was as if he took umbrage with my very existence. I briefly wondered if he hoped to purchase the cabin and keep the whole area to himself and my staying in the cabin hindered his plans.

I said, "Oh. Sorry."

"Married? Kids?"

"Me?"

He stared at me expectantly. I got the feeling I was being interrogated for some vile or malicious reason and I didn't feel comfortable answering his questions. I told myself the guy was one from the swarm of rednecks I'd encountered at The Pit Stop and would be a cantankerous asshole to anyone he thought threatened his right to his property or who might utter the words 'gun control'.

"No," I said.

His cruel half grin appeared and disappeared again. "A loner."

"Yes."

He grunted in such a way I wasn't sure if he was acknowledging my situation or mocking me. He pulled his hands from his pockets and crossed his arms again, concealing the scars, and looked around at my scattered belongings. "Well," he said. "I'll get goin' and let you get back to . . ." He took a few steps toward the door.

"Oh, sure."

I followed him to the door. If he wasn't such a peculiar character, throwing my instincts into warning mode, I would've insisted he stay until the rain passed or lightened. Instead I said, "If you ever need anything feel free to stop by." And the moment the words were out of my mouth I regretted it instantly.

71

He laid his hand on the frame of the screen door, peered over his shoulder at me, and said, "I'll be sure to do that. Be careful out here, boy." He tapped his temple and narrowed his vison on me. "The mind tends to play tricks when it's forced to be a companion to itself."

For a split second I swore I caught a glimpse of an evil intent and warning from him. Or maybe it was something else entirely. It wasn't something you could see on the surface or hear in his voice but something radiating from him. Something corrupt deep within his soul. He exuded dread and misery and, whatever it was, it gave me the sensation of a vicious undertow that could suck you into it like slipping into a warm bath. You would drown in it before you even knew the water was filling your lungs. I could browse a dictionary for days trying to find the words to describe how his presence made me feel but I don't think any of them could describe the wrongness radiating from the man. The guy creeped me the fuck out to the nth degree.

I nodded in answer and breathed a heavy sigh of relief when he slipped out the screen door and into the rain.

I closed the main door behind him and locked it before crossing the cabin and doing the same to the other door. I still didn't feel comfortable until I closed all the windows and had drawn the curtains shut. With everything closed the cabin was stuffy with heat and humidity. Something about Lloyd gave me the sensation of being watched and exposed even after I locked down the cabin against the outside. I tried to tell myself it was all in my head but I couldn't shake the feeling.

Something very bad happened in the exchange with Lloyd and I didn't know exactly what it was or how to describe it. I decided to call Phillip in the hopes he could somehow comfort me. I hoped talking with him would prove it was all in my head and his reassurance would make me realize I was overanalyzing the guy and the whole situation. I pulled the cellphone from my pocket but there was no reception.

I retrieved my laptop and nestled into the pile of blankets on the floor. My body was still sore and I knew getting back to my feet would be a chore. It took twenty minutes of fiddling with the wireless router program to get my computer connected to the Internet.

There was an email confirming a purchase of one of my framed photos. I groaned. I wanted the money from a paying customer but packaging up a photo and shipping it out felt like an exhausting task at the moment. There were more pressing matters I needed to tend to. I opened a new email and sent Phillip a rushed rehashing of the bizarre exchange with Lloyd. I asked him if he knew anything more about the neighbors. I wanted to know if Mom had told him anything other than they took out her trash when she was ill. I made sure to emphasize how creepy the guy was. I didn't want Phillip to think I was a whiny milquetoast who couldn't hack it on his own in the middle of the sticks so I omitted few things, but making sure to reiterate how a stranger entering my home when I wasn't there wasn't kosher with me.

When I was finished checking and sending emails I proceeded to research furniture stores in the area. There were only two. The same two I was able to pull up on my phone previously. One didn't have a website and the other store's site was littered with ill-lit photos of hideously overstuffed leather sofas and absurdly overpriced mattresses. I thought, *How can anyone afford to live on their own?*

My next Internet stop was craigslist. But the exceptionally rural area surrounding me was lacking in a decent selection and without renting a U-Haul and hiring someone to help me move the items or begging Phillip to come back and help me I was screwed. I resorted to knowing I wouldn't have a bed to sleep in tonight or maybe even within a week and searched for a discounted online store. I found one within a few hours of the cabin promising next day delivery. I signed up for their credit card to obtain the interest-free financing for a year and proceeded to hastily add items to the cart. When I was done I'd managed to snag a queen-size bed with a decent plain frame, a small dresser, a discontinued sofa in an inoffensive gray, a coffee table, a small black dinette table and chairs, and two wooden chairs for the deck because I never expected company other than Phillip periodically. I was pleased when I realized I hadn't managed to spend a third of what I'd imagined the cost would be. The quality of the furniture probably wasn't great but beggars couldn't be picky.

A notification appeared in the lower right-hand corner of my computer screen informing me I had two unread emails. I found a confirmation of my furniture order and a reply from Phillip. Phillip informed me he hadn't met the neighbors in person. Mom told him they'd helped her off and on but she didn't elaborate on them. All he knew about them was secondhand and that wasn't very much. He wrote off Lloyd's peculiar behavior to being a sheltered hillbilly. He was probably right. I wrote a brief response agreeing with him and informed him I would begin work on the cabin next week after I was settled.

My exchange with Phillip calmed me some. I closed my laptop and looked around the cabin. The pile of towels still needed to be washed but I didn't feel like dragging the pile down the steps while it was raining. I needed to shower and knew the hot water would soothe my worn muscles.

My legs ached when I rose and one of my feet had fallen asleep. I couldn't wait for the sofa to arrive. I dug through the boxes Phillip helped me move until I found the crappy pair of computer speakers Naomi gave me as a gift when I first moved in with her. She bought them for the office so I could listen to music while working on photos. I didn't have the heart to tell her I preferred headphones to block out everything when needed: the television show she was watching in the other room, the cupboard doors slamming as she retrieved a glass in the kitchen, the thudding of her feet down the hall on her way to the restroom. I plugged the speakers into my laptop, started a playlist, and adjusted the volume to a level that wasn't too offensive.

I retrieved the Tylenol bottle and took two before pulling one of the unwashed towels from the pile. I spent a long time under the hot water as I waited for the Tylenol to kick in. The water did wonders for my aches and pains and I let it run until it grew cold. I became frustrated after exiting the shower and having to deal with a new towel. It left traces of lint all over my body. I had to wait for my skin to air dry completely before brushing the lint off.

I continued with my normal grooming routine of shaving. I applied shaving cream to my face and lifted the razor but something caused me to stop short of applying the razor to my skin. What was the point in keeping a clean-cut appearance? I didn't need to impress anyone anymore. Naomi was the one who'd complain if my face was stubbly and she chose to remove herself from my life. I didn't have to shave if I didn't want to. I stared aimlessly at my own reflection for an undetermined amount of time, holding the razor inches from my face.

Staring at my reflection became hypnotic and my mind began to feel hazy and sluggish. Without a thought or hesitation I unscrewed the handle of my father's vintage razor and slipped the butterfly blade free of its holding. Thinking back on it, I couldn't have told you why I did what I did. I was moving under some other control. I was a marionette. But for the life of me I couldn't tell you who was pulling the strings or what their motive was. I held the blade between my thumb and forefinger and inspected the edge before placing the sharp corner of the blade against the flesh in the center of my chest. I pressed slowly until I felt the sting of blood being drawn. I began to carve a line. And once the first line was complete I cut another line and another. I was detached from my actions and performed them as if in a trance. I was apathetic to what I was doing to myself. Each stroke burned as the skin opened, blood welled in the incision, and spilled down my chest and stomach. I continued to cut in a mindless and natural action, like breathing. It felt like I was watching someone else, the pain a distant background sensation.

The blood flowed into my pubic hair and down the shaft of my penis. My cock stiffened with each cut and renewed dull flash of pain. I set the bloody razor on the counter and looked at the blood on my erection. I began to masturbate, using the blood as lubricant. I became fascinated with the sight of the blood on my penis and it didn't take long before I came. Most of the semen landed in the sink. I continued to stroke my cock. I looked at the shaving cream covering my face in the mirror and suddenly came to my senses.

What the fuck was I doing?

Blood dripped from my balls and padded softly on the floor. I immediately let go of my penis as if it had stung me. I looked at my blood-covered hand and chest, bewildered, as if waking from a dream. I frantically pulled the first-aid kit from below the sink. I was in a panic and didn't know what to do. There was so much blood. I decided my best bet was to take another shower to clean up.

I turned the shower on in a rush and stepped under a stream of freezing cold water. It swirled down the drain in streaks of red and pink. I adjusted the temperature but the hot water heater hadn't had time to warm the water. The cuts burned furiously when I cleaned them with soap and they continued to bleed. I was at a loss for how to staunch the flow. I resorted to ruining one of the new towels.

I cut the water and quickly retrieved the towel to press to my wound. I sat on the toilet and shivered. I crossed my arms to hold the towel to my chest and doubled over to apply pressure to the cuts. After a few minutes I rose to look at the wound in the mirror and gently pulled the towel away. Pieces of the towel and its lint stuck to the incisions. Removing the towel revealed a symbol I'd never seen before in the middle of my chest. It was approximately the size of my hand. I stared at it and the cuts slowly began to weep blood. I tried to gently blot the symbol with the towel and realized my hands were trembling. I opened the first-aid box and found the antibiotic ointment. I slathered it on the cuts and made a large bandage out of several packages of gauze. I had to stop a few times and take a deep breath and try to steady myself and keep from passing out.

When I was done I inspected the enormous white bandage speckled with growing dots of blood. I checked my reflection in the mirror and my eyes echoed the terror coursing through my veins. I touched the bandage on my chest and the wound stung.

There was the briefest moment when I thought of my father while I tried to rationalize what I'd done to myself. I thought of his death and everything his suicide delivered on our family and could only think of it as a curse. His mental health was a curse and I had inherited it. Everything I had just done was out of my control.

But I pulled myself out of those thoughts quickly. I couldn't blame my father for this. This was something different. There was a sensation filling my mind that said what I'd experienced was a disease. But it wasn't something I inherited from my father. It was something contagious. I had been infected with something unwanted that had crawled into my brain and made itself at home. There was a niggling in the back of my mind telling me Lloyd was the carrier.

I shook my head and touched the cuts again. I thought, *That's going to leave a scar.*

7

Sleep didn't come easy that night even with the assistance of a few beers. The burning from the cuts was a constant reminder of what I'd done. I was baffled by my actions and terrified to be alone. I never thought the day would come when I was scared of myself. I had inflicted the cuts upon my own flesh without flinching. What else was I capable of doing? Not only to myself but to other people. I thought of sending Phillip another message but I couldn't bring myself to type out the incident. I opened my laptop a couple of times and sat with an empty email open, cursor blinking, but the image of how I imagined Phillip would react kept me from sending him anything. I didn't want to worry him and it was probably something brought on by the stress of the breakup and the move and worrying about whether or not I could make enough money off my photos to sustain an existence out here in the middle of nowhere.

My thoughts kept drifting back to my father's suicide. Was

he aware of his actions in those last precious seconds of life? Did he tie a noose with an empty mind and flip the chair out beneath his feet without a second thought? He must have. It was the only sensible answer I could wrap my mind around. Because the alternative meant he premeditated the chaos he'd rained on our family. And if he had taken his own life with nothing but a mind full of apathy what did that say about what I'd done earlier? Had he harmed himself before he took his life? Only my mother would've known. And she made it clear early on after our father's death the subject was a taboo topic. Phillip and I had tiptoed around the topic and purposely made it a point to never mention him while Mom was around. I never knew if her intent was for the both of us to believe we were conceived out of thin air and never had a father in the first place but it was the unspoken agreement in our family to never talk about what had happened. And when an outsider or stranger mentioned our father to Mom in our presence her tone was tinged with haughtiness when she informed them he wasn't around anymore. Not around anymore. Not that he had taken his life but as if he'd chosen to leave his family or was abusive or a deadbeat and she'd eliminated him from our lives. Regardless, whatever knowledge Mom had known about Dad's death and the time leading up to it had gone to the grave with both of them. Because I had trouble remembering his face let alone how he acted. There were snippets of a handful of memories I could replay in my head but they were vague and distant and of a man who, with the passing of every day, grew more and more into a fading shadow and became a ghost. I couldn't remember anything out of the ordinary that would've signaled a warning but I was a kid then. And kids were nothing but narcissistic assholes only concerned with their own feelings which were superficial and survivalist as best: so and so won't give me my toy back, I hurt my knee, I'm hungry, I don't feel good.

I tossed and turned as the rain turned into a full-blown thunderstorm. The ruckus outside was accompanied by the sound of something I could only think of as a wailing animal in the distance. I wasn't sure if coyotes were indigenous to the area but the longer the animal carried on the more its cries began to sound human. After a while of desperately trying to fall asleep I opened my laptop and found a movie to watch for free. The flick wasn't something I was particularly interested in but I wanted to occupy my mind with something other than the cutting incident and my father's mental health and I desperately wanted to block out the sounds from outside and keep myself from Googling psychotic episodic symptoms until I was convinced I was either going crazy or had a brain tumor. The night was endless and the sensation I was waiting something out until the sun rose kept creeping into my thoughts. Like trying to keep someone who'd overdosed awake until the drug ran its course.

Eventually I managed to doze off near the end of the movie. But I slept fitfully and had a vivid dream of my father calling me, Phillip, and my mother into the living room of my childhood home. He had the three of us sit on the tired orange sofa with the wooden armrests and deflated and sagging cushions a small child could get sucked into. The same sofa Phillip and I had both managed to raise a decent sized goose egg lump on our heads from smacking our skulls on the wood when roughhousing. I was a kid again and so was Phillip. But Mom was older. And Dad stood in front of us. He smiled broadly even though his face was only a blur, and without a word, he pulled a small handgun from his back pocket. There was never a gun in our house while I was growing up and the sight of one fascinated and terrified me. My father lifted the gun to his temple and pulled the trigger. Streams of gold confetti erupted from his head and showered the living room.

I woke to a crack of thunder and was covered in sweat. Flashes of light filled the windows as the lightning did its ritual dance with the rain. The movie had ended on my laptop and the Internet site I used had randomly moved on to a clip of a heavyset man reviewing a cigarette vaping device he'd purchased. I closed the laptop.

The cabin was stifling with the windows and doors closed. I listened to the rain in the dark for a few minutes and the thunder rumble and decided I'd overreacted to Lloyd. I got out of my makeshift bed and cracked the windows to allow some fresh air to replace the suffocating stuffiness. I thought about pulling the cords for the ceiling fans but in the dark I couldn't be sure which cord was the right one and didn't want to be blasted by the light instead. I flipped the blankets around so the sweat-soaked sheets wouldn't be touching me before I lay back down. It didn't take me as long to fall asleep the second time.

When I woke in the morning the storm had passed. The sun shone brightly and the air was thick with humidity. I made breakfast and decided I needed to do laundry. I gathered the pile on the floor, including the bloodied towel from the bathroom. Out of habit I slipped my cellphone in my pocket before stepping outside. I was halfway down the stairs when my phone alerted me I had a voicemail. I continued down to the garage area and started the washer before checking my phone. There was no reception in the garage and the only spot I found a signal was on the stairs again. The message was from the furniture delivery people and I returned their call.

The man who answered sounded confused and disgruntled. "Who's calling?"

I said, "I have a voicemail asking me to return your call?"

"Lansing?"

"Yes."

The phone's earpiece emitted the sound of paperwork being shuffled and the rush of traffic.

The man made some uncertain sounds before he said, "Here it is. We have your furniture on the truck. Should be there . . . bout noon."

"Uh. Okay. It's sort of hard to find. My drive is steep and I have tiny turn around—"

He interrupted, angrily, "Been drivin' ten years. Ain't gonna be a problem. I think I can figure it out."

I didn't argue with him. I confirmed I'd be home for the delivery and climbed the stairs to the cabin. I spent the next hour moving things to make room for the furniture. The humidity caused me to sweat profusely and the cut on my chest stung as I worked.

A half an hour before the truck was scheduled to arrive I figured I should move my car out of the parking spot. I didn't know how large the truck was and I hoped it could use the parking area as a turnaround. I peered down at Lloyd's cabin and noticed the station wagon was gone. It also didn't appear he had any more room than I did for a delivery truck to maneuver.

I spotted movement in the doorway of his cabin. The main door was open and someone was watching from behind the screen door. The person retreated into the shadowy interior. I planned to pull my car out of the parking area and park it on the drive between the two cabins to allow the truck to use the parking space. I wasn't sure how long the delivery would take and the drive would be blocked the entire time. I figured I should mention it to whoever was at Lloyd's since the station wagon was missing and I didn't want to cause a mini traffic jam if they were returning soon.

I walked down the drive and climbed the steps to Lloyd's cabin. The steep incline behind his cabin kept the structure cooled by the shadows of the trees surrounding it. A damp chill saturated my skin as I stood in front of his door. I couldn't make out anything beyond the screen. I rapped on the wood frame of the screen door. A woman emerged from the shadows of the interior almost as if she'd materialized out of thin air. Her sudden appearance startled me. It was the same woman I'd seen the day I'd moved in. But she wasn't exactly a woman. If I was to guess her age based on the newness of her figure I would have picked maybe fifteen or sixteen. She was half a foot shorter than me and wore a thin cotton sun dress. I could see the pink skin of her areolas through the material. One of the nipples of her small breasts was hard. I averted my gaze and fought the urge to let my eyes explore further. I forced myself to look into her brown eyes because more blaring than her lack of undergarments was the ugly jagged scar across her neck. She was a pretty girl but there was something cruel and uncaring about her posture I couldn't quite figure out. My penis began to stiffen and I thought about the list of things I still needed from the store to distract myself from becoming aroused.

I stammered, regained myself, and said, "Is your dad home?"

Her eyes bounced to my chest and back up to meet mine. She said, "He's out." Her voice had a mature quality to it as if she had already seen and done too much in her life to qualify her as a teen. "He went to the store." One corner of her mouth twitched as if she were hiding a smirk.

A rustling and the slightest creak of wood came from within the darkness of the cabin. I couldn't see anything beyond her but I felt the presence of someone. Out of nowhere dread and fear gripped my throat and my mouth went dry. The image of a rabbit cowering in the brush as a wolf caught its scent came to mind. Something primitive inside my head screamed danger as the faintest movement of air passed through the screen door carrying a scent I could only describe as a blend of decaying leaves and clove.

"Well, I . . ." I said. I took a step back and thumbed over my shoulder to indicate my car. "I have a delivery truck arriving soon and we might block the drive. Do you know when he'll be back?"

She slipped one hand inside a hidden pocket on her dress and pushed open the screen door at the same time. I backed away and put a few feet between us as she stepped out onto the porch, barefoot. The rustling sound within the cabin faded as if it were receding toward the back of the structure. She produced a pack of unfiltered cigarettes and a lighter from her pocket. I bit back the urge to ask her if she was old enough to smoke. She lit a cigarette and dropped the lighter and pack back into her pocket before she answered.

She said, "He probably won't be back for another hour or so." She took a pull of her cigarette, crossed one arm under her breasts, pulling the material of her dress tighter and making her nipples more visible, and balanced the elbow of her cigarette holding hand in the palm of her other hand. She observed me with an air of amusement. "So . . . what do you do?"

The question struck me as odd. It was a question one adult would ask another. Not a question a teenager would ask or be bothered to want to know or care about the answer.

In my peripheral I could see the small dark patch of her pubic hair beneath her dress. I blinked and focused on the smoke of her cigarette and thought, *Laundry basket, aluminum foil, insect repellant* . . . I said, "I'm a photographer."

"Nature? Like . . . birds and stuff?" She twirled her cigarette holding hand to insinuate the trees around us. Simultaneously she stuck out the tip of her pink tongue and brought her free hand to her mouth. She plucked a small piece of tobacco from her tongue before recrossing her arm beneath her breasts.

"People. Black and white photos mainly."

"Cool." She nodded approvingly and took another puff of her cigarette. She lightly tapped her cigarette with her index finger to rid it of its ashes.

She genuinely seemed interested in the subject. Maybe I'd pegged her wrong. Maybe she wasn't just another teenager. Maybe she was really interested in the arts. I was engrossed in photography when I was her age and it gave me pleasure to know a handful of other kids my age were interested in creating something and we all had lofty ambitions and hopes of becoming celebrities who were adored and we wanted our creations to be fawned over by millions of adoring and admiring fans. But more often than not, if I happened to stumble into those same people again as adults and brought up the subject of their photography or painting or writing or whatever art they were passionate about as a teen, they would give a dry laugh and inform me they gave it up years ago because now they had a career that actually gave them a paycheck and a litter of children who required all their attention and a partner who'd rather sit around and talk about their daily woes every night after supper and they'd decided it wasn't worth it to fight for a free moment to work on the thing they were so passionate about all those years ago. It was refreshing to find someone who actually might give a shit about my photography.

I said, "You're more than welcome to take a look at them sometime."

I regretted saying it before I'd finished the sentence. I couldn't help myself. I kept glancing at the scar on her neck and it screamed for attention. It screamed to be photographed. The scar wanted its story to be told. Or I wanted to make it into something people would look at and struggle with the meaning behind it. I kept thinking of what lighting I would use and what angle and how I would crop the photo when it was finished. The desire to photograph certain things always grew into a gnawing sensation of want. But those models answered an ad and knew what they were stepping into. And I'd never enforced an age limit. I had taken and sold photos of children born with deformities with written consent from their parents. But I'd never approached a stranger before and pointed out their blaring flaw and asked them if I could capture something that could possibly be their utmost insecurity on film and magnify it for a profit. Sure, they received a one-time payment for modeling but they had stumbled onto one of my ads and had made the decision to approach me. Talking to her about her scar shortly after meeting and telling her about my fetish seemed gauche. Especially since she was so young. I had no idea how she would react if she saw the collection of photos. Not to mention I was sure Lloyd wouldn't be thrilled about his daughter visiting my cabin alone. And the last thing I wanted was for Lloyd to be pissed off at me or, even less desirable, for him to accompany her.

She snapped me out of my reverie. She pointed to my chest and said, "You've got something on your shirt." She smirked and took another draw of her nearly spent cigarette.

I looked down to see the self-inflicted cuts had seeped through the bandages and a couple small spots of blood had absorbed into my shirt. I struggled to come up with an explanation but only stammered. The whine of a large engine descending the drive drew both of our attentions. A box truck creeped around the sharp corner of the drive.

"I'm sorry," I said. "I have to move my car. I hope it doesn't inconvenience your dad."

I took the stairs unceremoniously. My nervousness made my legs wobbly. I jogged toward the truck and almost tripped when I discreetly tried to inspect the blood on my shirt. The slap of the screen door behind me startled me as if it were a gun blast.

8

I spent a half an hour directing the self-proclaimed professional driver of the moving truck in a fifty-point turn around. I could tell the man was growing more and more agitated with me by the deepening of his scowl as he glared at me through the windshield of his truck and by the shrinking posture of his young and quiet companion. I knew nothing of driving a truck or how to direct it. My mind was more focused on getting the furniture off the truck before Lloyd returned to find himself blocked from his own home and no way to turn around. I didn't want to have any more interactions with Lloyd if I could help it.

Once the truck was situated I helped to relieve the two of the furniture haul to move things along quicker. The young delivery guy eyed me dubiously after scrutinizing the stains on my shirt. I followed his gaze and apologized and told him I'd had a nose bleed earlier. I was certain he could make out the puffy patch of bandages under my shirt and I avoided any more conversation with either of them. The two men sweated heavily as they unloaded the truck.

When we were finished I gave them each a bottle of water and handed them each twenty dollars as a tip that didn't feel adequate. Both of the men's hard demeanors visibly softened with the newly gained cash. Even with little money to give I couldn't bring myself to stiff them on a tip. My job at the café made me appreciate the people who could spare a dollar if nothing else. If you were willing to pay fifteen dollars for an oversized coffee drink that was more milk and sugar and syrupy flavoring than actual coffee and top it off with extra whipped cream and a scone the size of your head then you could afford to drop your server a dollar. Tipping someone who provided a service was the socially responsible thing to do since hourly wages for those jobs were a joke and any one person could not afford a living off a single job paying minimum wage. I knew it made *me* resentful when a customer showed up wearing name brand apparel and designer shoes and sneered at me as if I'd pulled out my penis and began jerking off while I prepared their order and they walked off without even glancing at the tip jar once I handed them their drink.

I was relieved once the movers were on their way. Ten minutes after they were gone I recognized the crunch of gravel from outside and imagined it was the sound of Lloyd's station wagon as it passed my cabin.

The next hour consisted of deconstructing the makeshift bed on the floor to make the new bed and folding clothes and arranging them in the dresser. I followed the nesting routine with packing the photo a customer purchased for shipping, making a list of other items I needed from the store, and researching the nearest post office online. There was a small town with a post office closer than the town with the supercenter store. But the post office and a gas station were the only things located in the aforementioned town other than a few scattered houses. I chose to make the extra drive to the city so I could pick up a few forgotten things.

I showered and soaked the tape of the makeshift bandage with water to make its removal easier. The wound was hot to the touch but appeared to have stopped seeping for the moment and hadn't formed a scab yet. The skin around each cut was an angry red and I tried to remember when the last time I had had a tetanus shot was. Once I was out of the shower I cleaned the area with rubbing alcohol, which burned like hell and made my teeth feel like they were vibrating when I clenched my jaw against the pain. I decided to let the cuts breathe before applying another bandage. I took the opportunity to try out the bed. I lay on the bed, naked, watching the ceiling fan turn lackadaisically and listening to the birds singing outside.

My thoughts wandered to the girl at Lloyd's cabin and her breasts and the small patch of darkness between her legs and I found myself becoming aroused. I told myself I didn't have time to masturbate. Besides, I'd never learned her name and didn't have any idea how old she was and the fact I was becoming aroused while thinking about her disturbed me. She had smoked a cigarette but that didn't mean anything about her age. Just because it wasn't legal to smoke under the age of eighteen didn't mean it wasn't possible. I was certain she was underage and it made me feel disgusted with myself and guilty for finding her arousing. I was probably twice her age.

I reminisced back to a time when I was thirteen and smoked my first cigarette. Mom managed to procure a tiny worn down house in a decent school district. I didn't make many friends at school because by the age of thirteen I was on to Mom's inability to make enough money for us to stay anywhere too long. But there were two kids in my class, Zack and Nate, who didn't seem to be bothered by my sudden appearance in their class at the start of the school year and were probably just as apathetic about my disappearance nine months later when an eviction notice appeared on our door. Phillip had reached the age of coolness where he was no longer interested (correction, he was downright *embarrassed*) in walking with me to school because there were girls to ogle and a driver's license to dream about. A few weeks after starting the new school I began to meet Zack and Nate a few blocks from my house in the morning. We walked together and the other two would talk about movies or video games as I listened and wished for the day when Mom might be able to afford a game console or I would be old enough to get a summer job and buy one for myself. I don't remember much about that time other than being chagrined about my situation and hoping for a lot of things that would never come without my volition. On one unremarkable day Zack had found an unmolested cigarette on the sidewalk before he'd met me and Nate. I couldn't remember the reason Nate gave for having a book of contraband matches in his backpack but it didn't take us long before we found a hiding spot behind someone's garage and the three of us lit the cigarette and passed it around. Once the coughing fits and dizziness subsided we continued on to school. I got sick shortly after our arrival. I can still conjure the fretful expression Mom wore when she picked me up from the nurse's office. Till today I don't know if she was more worried about my wellbeing or the loss of hours from her job. The latter was more likely. And I never had the urge to smoke again after puking my brains out.

I cleared my head of the memory of smoking my first cigarette and of Lloyd's daughter and returned to the bathroom. I used the last of the gauze to make a loose bandage, made a mental note to buy more, and dressed.

On the way to the post office I noticed a house not too far from my own with a large wooden structure split into squares. It appeared to be an oversized storage structure stuffed with split logs. Each sectioned square was one of two different sizes and numbers were spray painted above each section. I imagined the numbers were the price of the lot of wood. There was a small sign by the road with the word 'firewood' spray painted on it. I didn't recall seeing any wood at the cabin, and knew it was early in the summer and I wouldn't need it for a while, but I thought it would be a good idea to be prepared for any unseasonably cool nights. I also wanted to find out if they could deliver. There was no way for me to take it myself without loading it in the trunk of my car.

I continued on to the post office and picked up some more first-aid items and a few other stray things I'd forgotten. On my way back home I stopped at the house with the firewood sign.

The house was what one would think of when asked to conjure an image of a farmhouse. It was a white two-story structure with faded and chipped white paint. The house had a covered front porch with two large wooden rocking chairs positioned to look out over the lawn stretching toward the road. The main door was open and through the screen door came the muffled sounds of cheering from a television set. I knocked on the screen door. There was a pregnant silence and I was about to knock a second time when I heard shuffling. I was greeted by an elderly hunchback woman in a cotton dress with a floral pattern and pink slippers that made a scuffing sound when she walked. Her white hair was pulled into a bun and she wore an oversized pair of glasses. A twang of disappointment hit me once I recognized how feeble she was. There was no way this woman, or her husband, could deliver the wood. The old woman pushed open the screen door a few inches to talk to me.

She said, "Can I help you?"

"Yes," I said. I thumbed over my shoulder at the firewood. "I would like to buy some firewood but I don't have a way to haul it."

"Oh," she said. "That's no problem. My son can deliver for an extra ten dollars."

"That would be great."

She pushed the door open farther and said, "He's at work right now. But if you want I can take down your address and number. He'll call you to set up a time."

I nodded and she motioned for me to enter the house. She led me through a darkened living room lined with overstuffed brown leather furniture and brown carpet and cheap imitation wood paneling. The walls were covered with old and worn photos of people I assumed were family members. The room was illuminated by the faint sunlight trickling through the sheer curtains and the glow of a television airing a daytime gameshow. I followed her into a brightly lit kitchen with an old Formica topped table with worn red vinyl covered chairs. A napkin holder sat in the middle of the table along with a small notepad and pen. She handed me the latter two and I wrote down my name, address, and number, being careful to print it neatly so it could be read easily. I was used to scribbling down things only I could decipher. When I was done I handed her the note pad, reached into my back pocket, retrieved my wallet, and thumbed through the bills.

"You never mind that," she said. She looked at what I'd written, squinted, and simultaneously said, "You pay Charles when he delivers." Her expression changed into one of surprise as she read the notepad. "Oh!"

"Is there a problem?" I stowed my wallet in my back pocket.

The old woman looked at me. "You moved into Karen's old cabin?"

"She was my mother."

She made a clucking noise and shook her head. "Was a shame to hear about her passing. Your mama was a nice lady. Used to stay and drink a cup of coffee with me when she placed her order." She waved her hand dismissively at me and smiled with a touch of nostalgia. "We'd gossip about those peculiar characters down the road from her like a couple of school girls."

"She told you about those two?"

The old woman held up three fingers.

"Three?" I said.

She nodded over animatedly. She gave a dry little laugh and laced the fingers of her hands together. "Don't listen to me.

Your mama was creative with those tall tales. I let her pull my leg all the time. I don't get many visitors and I let people go on and on for a little bit of company. People 'round here come up with all kinds of stories about the local hermits."

"What did she tell you?"

"Oh." Her face flushed. "Mostly about what she heard coming from the cabin late at night. Said she was certain the father was having an *inappropriate* relationship with that girl." She raised her eyebrows as if to question whether I understood what she was insinuating.

"Uhf," was all I managed to get out. A sickening chill ran up my spine and a pang of disgust emanated deep in the pit of my stomach.

"She also had some crazy tales about a tall creature who ran around . . . *nude* in the woods at night. She said it lived with those people."

"Creature?"

"Honey, don't you worry yourself about all that cockamamie. Old wives' tales. People been hollerin' about creatures in the woods for as long as I can remember. Sasquatch and wolf men and deformed inbred lunatics. It's all malarkey." She tapped her temple with the corner of the note pad. "And sometimes being a shut-in for too long can play tricks on the mind."

She tapped my chest with the notepad, hitting the cuts on my chest. The pain renewed and I fought the urge to wince or grab her hand to stop her.

"You never mind those stories," she said sternly. "They're old spook stories to give the kiddies night terrors."

"Did you ever meet her neighbors?"

She placed the notepad on the kitchen table. "No. They don't buy firewood from us." She slowly took a seat at the table. "Would you like to stay for a bit? I could make some coffee or tea."

A part of me wanted to know more about what my mother told her. It was out of character for my mother to make up stories about monsters in the woods. And she must have heard something or seen something terrible to make such a vile accusation about Lloyd and his daughter. It struck me as odd she didn't tell Phillip anything more than they had taken out her trash if she suspected they were committing such terrible acts.

The elderly woman appeared lonely and in want of a gossiping companion. I did want to know everything my mother told her but I had some grocery items in my car and I didn't exactly feel comfortable or believe what the woman was saying. There were only two people living in the other cabin that I was aware of. It was more likely the old woman had my mother mixed up with someone else or the stories she was eluding to were constructed of her own imagination. Or delusions brought on by the onset of a mentally deteriorating disease.

"No, thank you though. I have some things in my car I need to refrigerate."

"Maybe another time?"

I nodded. "Sure. Another time." I knew I was only placating her. I would probably never return until I needed more firewood.

"All right then," she said.

I said my goodbyes and she reassured me her son would call that evening. I informed her my phone didn't have the greatest reception and told her to tell her son to leave a message if I didn't answer. I left with a headful of dreadful images and questions about Lloyd and his daughter and whatever might be lurking in the woods. I tried to tell myself none of it was real but I couldn't remember a time when my mother lied about something so ridiculous if the woman could be believed and my mother had been the one telling the stories. The lies Mom constructed about our financial situation while Phillip and I were kids was one thing. She was protecting us from unnecessary adult worries and taking on the burden and stress herself. She never tried to appease us with superfluous nonsense stories or bedtime fables. If it were true, if Mom had been the one originating the tales, this was something completely different and out of character for her.

9

Charles scheduled and delivered the wood two days later. He was a bulky man with a thick head of hair and a full beard. He was tall and sun-worn and well-muscled and appeared as though he was constructed out of the obvious life-long hard labor he'd supported himself with. He smelled like grease and sweat and mint. He asked the customary standard questions about me and where I was from and what I did when he delivered the wood. He was reluctant to carry on the conversation once I mentioned the photography and I didn't blame him. The people in the area seemed to interpret an invasion of outsiders, aside from the constant stream of tourists, with an air of reluctance and suspicion. I chalked up the majority of Charles' ill feelings about me to my straggly and fledgling beard. I was sure he viewed me as some type of lumberjack or hillbilly poser who claimed to be an artist from the city who'd moved to the wilderness to get in touch with nature and take some photos. In reality, I was poor and this was the cheapest way for me to live on my own and not be a burden to someone else until I could come up with enough money to find a place I could afford on my own. I was thirty and newly single. Why else would I choose to move here? There were tons of women and opportunities for models and making money in the city in comparison to the middle of nowhere. And when I really stopped to think about it I still clung to a bare thread of hope Naomi would change her mind even though I hated to admit it. Living somewhere in the city made me easily accessible to Naomi and there was a possibility I could run into her at our normal haunts had I chose to stay with Phillip. Monotony and routine were comfortable. Starting anew sucked. And I had to face the fact I was too lazy and too tired to play the dating game anymore. What could I possibly offer a woman at this point? Flakiness? No money? No prospects? An aging man who refused to become the all-American male with two kids, a house, a respectable job with a trophy wife, and two brand new cars in the garage topped off with a big screen television to watch sports on mindlessly after working his ass off at a job he hated?

I helped Charles haul the wood in armloads down the bisected flights of stairs. My first armload was piled high and the wood scraped against the cuts on my chest. Charles pointed out where my mother used to stack her supply of wood. There was a cubby under the deck stairs beside the house I hadn't paid much attention to before. We found the remnants of her last winter's woodpile covered by a battered blue tarp. I inconspicuously checked the wound on my chest once I'd dropped the firewood on the stack to make sure I hadn't disrupted the scabbing and caused it to bleed again. There was no blood and I silently reprimanded myself to be more careful.

I asked Charles questions he probably viewed as dumb but I'd never used a fireplace before. I was used to a digital thermostat on the wall and the one time I'd received any trouble out of the electric furnace Naomi called the landlord. I expected Charles to be more condescending than he actually was. He explained to me the best way to start and run the fireplace. He also advised me to hire someone to clean the chimney since I didn't know the last time it was done. He gave me a phone number for a friend who was a chimneysweep as a side job for extra cash. We located the fire poker and broom set which doubled as a stand to hold a small pile of wood in the garage area beneath the cabin.

Once we were finished I offered him a beer but he politely declined and said he had to be on his way. I tried to give him an extra twenty dollars for explaining everything to me but he declined it also. I decided to follow him as he took his leave and make sure we hadn't dropped anything deemed dangerous to car tires.

Charles' line of sight kept narrowing in on the other cabin as he approached his truck. I glanced down the way and didn't see anyone on the porch and the station wagon was parked in its normal spot.

Charles opened his truck door and I approached him before he shut it.

I nodded toward the other cabin. "What do you know about them?"

"Nothing really. I've never delivered to them."

He lifted a can of chewing tobacco from the console of his car, retrieved a large pinch, and placed it in his lower lip. I noticed a spent plastic soda bottle in the console which appeared to hold the contents of his wasted spit and chew.

"Must have electric heat," he said. "Never seen any smoke from their chimney when deliverin' to Miss Karen."

I responded with a nod and glanced at the cabin. The girl appeared on the porch. I hadn't heard the slap of their screen door and her sudden materialization startled me. She watched us and lifted a lighter to the cigarette dangling from her mouth.

Charles lowered his voice as if he were afraid the girl would hear us. "Weird folk," he said. "Don't see the girl anywhere but on that porch." He inclined his head slightly in her direction. "Neither one of 'em work 'round here. People tell crazy stories about 'em."

I kept my voice low and conspiratorial, much like his. "Your mom told me they, uh . . ." I was reluctant to say the word incest or to imply such a harsh accusation. The people in this area must know the stigma that comes with living rural and I didn't want any of them to take offense or misinterpret what the 'city boy' had insinuated.

Charles finished my thought. "Rumor has it the ol' man keeps his daughter under tight watch and has his way with her."

I cleared my throat. "Do you know her name? I had a brief conversation with the man when I moved in. Said his name was Lloyd. He didn't mention her name."

"One of the girls who worked at The Pit Stop says her name is Tryphena. Says she talked to them when they first moved here."

"How long ago was that?"

"Oh." He lifted the soda bottle from a holder in the console, held it to his lips, and spat brown slime into the container. He held the bottle but sat it on his thigh. "Probably 'bout six or seven years ago. Laura, the girl from The Pit Stop, said the girl hadn't quite hit puberty then. You know?" He cupped his free hand in front of his chest to insinuate large breasts.

I fought the urge to shudder at his vulgar gesture for prepubescent. "Yeah," I said, hoping my response would prompt him to stop.

He dropped his hand. "Laura said the father gave her the heebie-jeebies. Said he didn't treat the girl right. Real handsy with her. Caressing her hair and bein' an all-around weirdo."

I highly doubted a word of his story was true. I'd stopped in The Pit Stop. The staff appeared less than friendly or in the mood to strike up a conversation with a stranger and prod them for information. I surely didn't have a conversation with any of the folks on my first visit. They most likely assumed I was another one of the tourists or any other new face moseying through the store. Besides, even if Lloyd and his daughter had a conversation with one of the employees years ago the accusation of incest was one of speculation and not based on any hard evidence. I hoped if someone made such a claim the police would've gotten involved.

"No one's seen her in public since," he said.

"What about school?"

He shrugged. "Must've homeschooled."

He deposited another glob of spit in the soda bottle. I glanced at the cabin. The girl crushed her cigarette and retreated back into the cabin. The screen door punctuated her leave with a slap.

"Damn shame," Charles said. "Pretty thing."

"I don't think she's old enough to smoke."

"Kids 'round here ain't old enough to do a lot of things. But they still do 'em since they got nothin' else to keep 'em occupied."

We both stared at the other cabin in silence.

Charles broke his reverie. "Well." He placed his hand on the handle of the truck door. "I ought to get goin'. The missus has a honey-do list a mile long."

I took a step back and gave him room to shut his door. "Sure thing. Thanks for everything. I really appreciate it."

With his hand still on the handle he nodded at me. "Don't forget to give Dale a call about cleanin' the chimney before you use it."

I patted my pocket where I stowed the paper with the phone number. "Will do."

He pulled the truck door shut. I retreated to the top of the stairs and watched him as he turned his mammoth truck around. He gave a quick bleat of his horn as he headed back down the trail and toward the incline. I waved and waited until he was out of sight before I descended the stairs.

10

Over the next couple of weeks I worked on the floors of the cabin. The first thing I tried to do was remove the few stains located in the inconspicuous areas. I took to the Internet for tips and home remedies. It took a couple of applications to see an improvement. I also cleaned the whole floor thoroughly two times to eliminate the dog odor.

Renting the floor sander was the challenging part of the whole project. A day's rental cost me nearly fifty dollars and the damn thing weighed a hundred pounds. An employee at the store helped me load the contraption into the trunk of my car but I didn't have anyone to help me once I arrived home.

I debated approaching Lloyd for assistance once I arrived home with the machine. I sat in the car and stared at his cabin but my ego wouldn't allow me to admit to another man I was weak. But honestly, I didn't want to talk to him because he'd creeped me out during the little interaction we'd had.

I managed to wrestle the sander out of the car by myself and knew once I was finished with the day's work I was going to be sore. I carried the sander from the car to the top of the stairs before setting it down and taking a short break. I stopped every couple of stairs and tried not to rest too long between moving the machine. I wouldn't allow fatigue to set in and pushed myself until I'd carried the damn thing all the way down to the door.

Once I was in the house with the sander I drank a glass of water and looked at the furniture. I partly regretted not holding off buying furniture until after the floors were finished but I was too old to sleep on the floor for more than a day or two. I wished I'd had enough money to rent the sander for a couple of days but my bank account told me it wasn't an option. The sales of my photographs were steady enough to provide for myself. Most of the population lived paycheck to paycheck and were paid a steady amount on a weekly or bi-weekly basis. I lived from day to day and never knew when I would get paid next or when interest in my work would come to a screeching halt.

I mustered up the energy and pushed my physical endurance by moving all of the furniture out the back door and onto the covered deck. I reconstructed the bed, knowing I would have to sleep on the deck for a couple of days. I'd already debated doing the floor in two halves but the weather was hot during the day and cool at night. I hadn't noticed too many mosquitoes as of yet and could always sleep with a blanket over my head to ward off the pesky blood suckers if they decided to make a feast out of me. Besides, I didn't want a four day project to turn into eight and be without access to the restroom and kitchen during the day for the same amount of time.

Once the furniture was moved I promptly sanded the floors, wrestled the sander back up the stairs and into the trunk, cleaned the floors to make sure every speck of dust was gone, and took a steaming hot shower to ease my already aching body. I knew once I woke up tomorrow I would feel like I'd been hit by a truck.

I inspected the newly formed scars on my chest in the mirror once I was out of the shower. Most of the scabs had fallen off. The cuts healed into a pink design of scarred flesh. I touched the tender skin and inspected my now reasonable looking beard. I had to put the unusual incident of self-mutilation out of my head and knew I would have to fabricate a story to explain the scar once I was in another relationship.

The day had grown into darkness by the time I was done with my shower. I made a mental list as I dressed in a fresh set of clothes. I tried to think of what food items I could keep on the deck for the next few days. Using the woods as a toilet wasn't ideal but would be necessary and remembering a roll of toilet tissue was top priority before I started on the floor. The polyurethane took twenty-four hours to dry in between coats and the floors would need three coats. I would only have access to the bathroom and kitchen once a day after each coat dried and before applying the next. I deliberated applying the first layer before turning in but I was too exhausted. I would wait until tomorrow and afterward I would return the sander to kill some time.

I took a couple of Tylenol and sat on the deck and drank a couple of beers while checking and responding to emails. I contemplated masturbating after mindlessly clicking over to a porn site but my body felt like Jell-O from the physical exertion of the day. Instead I drank my beer and watched an entire video of a waifish girl with long brunette hair being strapped onto an unusually short table by two men. The table had two braces to keep her legs spread and her head hung over the table so she viewed everything upside down. One of the men inserted a type of gag into the girl's mouth that fastened behind her head. The gag wasn't a normal ball gag. It was fashioned with two metal brackets that held the girl's mouth open as if she were a patient being prepped for dental surgery. One of the men disrobed and began fucking her cunt while the other man held the back of the girl's head and fucked her mouth. The man screwing her mouth pinched the nipples of her small breasts hard while he fucked her. She gagged constantly and her slobber ran from her mouth in long ropey streams toward the floor. At one point the men switched. The man who'd previously fucked her pussy had a larger penis than the first and he didn't waste any time jackhammering the girl's mouth while gripping both sides of her head to keep her steady. The girl's whole body convulsed and her stomach muscles clenched as she gagged. The man screwing her cunt proclaimed her pussy felt good as it tightened around his cock when she gagged. The man screwing her vaginally finally withdrew his penis, jerked off on her stomach, and disappeared from the frame. The other man continued to fuck the girl's mouth relentlessly. She made sounds of protest. Even if there were a safe word the girl was unable to speak it. The man who'd already came reappeared within the frame of the video with a massive dildo the size of his forearm. Without ceremony he drove the dildo into the girl's pussy and began vigorously fucking her with it. The man fucking the girl's mouth suddenly withdrew his penis and the camera closed in on him masturbating furiously in front of the girl's tear, snot, and saliva streaked face. There was a terrified look in the girl's eyes as she gasped for air through her stretched mouth. The man finally ejaculated. The first spurt hit the girl in the chin and started to run down toward her mouth. The man moved in closer and the second wave of semen landed directly in the girl's mouth. The third squirt landed in her mouth but trailed down her cheek and mingled with her drool and snot. The man's penis emitted a couple more pumps that only ran over the head of his cock and onto his hand.

I watched the entire video in fascination at the girl's ability to submit to being nothing more than a lump of flesh with two holes meant as a means of fulfillment for someone else. At the end the video the girl was unstrapped, given a towel to clean up, and the video cut to an after interview of the girl describing how she found the whole episode sexually pleasing because in her mind pleasure and pain went hand in hand.

I closed my laptop and finished the last swallow of my beer. I was painfully horny and regretted watching the porno. My arms were sore and I was too exhausted to jerk off but I knew I would anyway. And I wasn't sure if I was more aroused from watching the porno or from the girl's nonchalant addition at the end about getting off sexually from pain. When I thought back to the cutting incident I knew the feeling of pain was part of what turned me on.

The woods beyond the light of the deck were completely enveloped in the blackness of night. I stood and approached the railing, feeling every ounce of the alcohol I'd consumed and the loose ache of my muscles. I checked the night sky and didn't see the moon and wondered if it was a new moon or beyond the roof of the cabin and out of my line of sight. I unfastened my shorts, slid my hand into my underwear, and slowly started stoking myself. I pushed my underwear down far enough to expose my cock and balls. My shorts fell around my ankles. I was unsteady from the beer and held the railing with one hand while masturbating with the other. I closed my eyes and pictured Tryphena's face in place of the girl's in the video. I pictured my dick as the one fucking her mouth with the same pace as my stroking. And then I pictured the scar on her throat. I replaced the image of fucking her mouth with one of me slitting her throat where her scar was and forcing my cock into her esophagus through the cut and fucking her blood-spurting neck. The imagery sent me over quickly.

I let out an involuntary yelp when I came.

The orgasm was intense and almost painful. My legs threatened to give out and I clung to the railing firmly. I opened my eyes to see the second shot of semen arch over the railing and into the darkness of the night. And much like the man in the video, the last of my orgasm spilled over my hand. I let go of my penis and held the railing with both hands as I regained my composure.

I was stunned by the spontaneous imagery I'd conjured in the fantasy. The fact I was able to think of such a thing was repulsive and made me feel shameful.

I took a couple of deep breaths and stared at the thin line of semen as it stretched from the tip of my withering dick and made its way to the deck. I tucked my penis back into my underwear and wiped my hand off on the inside of my underwear. I pulled my shorts back up and a tiny light in the darkness of the woods caught my attention. I peered over the railing and it took me a few seconds to register there were two lights and the lights were the reflection of the porch light off animal eyes. The set of eyes was close to the cabin and appeared enormous. I couldn't be sure, but from my viewpoint the animal appeared tall. I didn't know if it was a trick of the light or my inebriated state but it appeared taller than a person. Its entire body was enveloped in the darkness and I couldn't make out a silhouette. I hoped it was a deer but worried it might be a bear. And then suddenly the lighted eyes were gone. Blinked out. I listened carefully for the scuttling of an animal and figured I would be able to identify it by its gait. I heard nothing. Only the trill of a few insects.

I decided it might be best for me to sleep with one of the kitchen knives. Just in case.

11

The first night I slept on the deck without incident. I was too exhausted and probably would have slept through a bear eating me. I woke up stiff and sore from head to toe but I pushed myself to make breakfast and apply the first coat of polyurethane to the floor.

After the first coat was applied I returned the floor sander and spent the rest of the day in town. I found the library and theater and wasted time at both before eating a late supper. I stopped and bought a small cooler, ice, and beer before heading home.

I spent the evening on the deck checking messages and looking up videos of how to remove the kitchen cabinets and replace them. I would need help getting them up the stairs and into the cabin. Especially the countertop. I sent Phillip an email asking if he could come out and help me when he had a free day.

Two emails appeared in my inbox for photograph orders,

which boosted my mood. I had to rearrange the crowded deck to get to the photos and packaged them for shipment.

A few bugs began to bother me as they fluttered around the light by the door. Once I didn't need the light for assistance I figured it would be best to shut it off so I wouldn't be eaten by whatever winged creatures it attracted. I drank a few beers in the darkness and was accompanied by my thoughts and the sounds of the night insects. Eventually I grew tried and turned in.

My dreams were chaotic and unintelligible. In the night something smacked my face and began lightly stroking my cheek. The sensation was scratchy and I woke in a panic. I flailed and yelped, searching for the knife. It took a few seconds of thrashing about and trying to produce the knife before I came to my senses and abandoned the bed. I opened the back door and flipped on the outside light and prepared to fight whatever had attacked me with my bare hands. I squinted against the sudden brightness and faced my attacker. A black shiny object the size of my thumb crawled across my pillow. I hesitantly stepped closer to inspect the largest beetle I'd ever laid eyes on. It had enormous pinchers and appeared prehistoric. The bug suddenly took flight. It flew directly into the side of the cabin and produced a sound like snapping plastic and fell to the deck. It landed on its back and buzzed furiously as it fluttered its wings and tried to right itself.

"Jesus," I said.

My heart raced with the sudden jolt from sleep to the fear my life was in danger. I found a pen and flicked the beetle off the edge of the deck. I waited a couple of minutes for the bug to come flying back with a vengeance, like an angered bee, before I deemed it safe enough to urinate over the railing. My bladder was threatening to burst when I decided the coast was clear. Urine pattered on the ground below. Halfway through urinating a sound in the distance provoked me to worry the beetle would return, land on my dick, and pinch me. I tried to hurry.

As I finished the sound came again in the distance. I thought it sounded like a long drawn out whine from an animal. But then it became erratic and it took a couple of minutes to realize it was coming from the front side of the cabin. I checked the time on my cellphone. It was a couple of minutes after three A.M. A single bar of reception on my phone disappeared and a small notification box popped up on the screen informing me I didn't have a signal.

I shut the light off for the deck and waited a few minutes for my eyes to adjust to the darkness. The noise came in infrequent intervals and varied in intensity. Once I was able to make out the shadows of the furniture I slipped on my shoes—making sure to shake them in case some insect decided to make them its new home—and I walked around the side of the cabin and toward the front. The noise came again as I carefully climbed the stairs to the drive.

At the top of the stairs I stared at Lloyd's cabin and tried to put together why his lights would flicker irregularly. He had lacey white curtains and the light made them glow a soft yellow-orange. It dawned on me if his cabin had a similar layout to mine and he also had a fireplace he may have his lit. Maybe the reason Lloyd didn't get firewood delivered was because he cut his own. But the night was fairly warm and I couldn't see why anyone would waste the time or resources lighting a fire. I could only imagine the heat it would produce would be stifling. While staring at his house and contemplating the dancing lights in Lloyd's window the sound came again. It was definitely coming from his cabin. At this distance it no longer sounded like an animal but a woman's wail.

An uneasy sensation ran down my spine and goosebumps rose on my arms. I looked up at the night sky. The moon was half full and there were no clouds. I don't know what compelled me but I began to make my way toward his cabin. Whatever was happening inside was none of my business. And, if I had to admit it, I was afraid of Lloyd. The last thing I wanted was for him to catch me lurking around his place. He struck me as a man who owned a shotgun and would be happy to find someone trespassing on his property so he could shoot them first and ask questions later. But I had to know what the noise was. And a force I'd never experienced before scratched the word 'destiny' into the synapses of my brain and terrified me. The same force pulled me toward Lloyd's and told me I had to see for myself.

I used the scant moonlight to find my way along the drive, sticking to the grassy area along the side to avoid disturbing the gravel and making noise. Once I was close I tiptoed across the gravel drive to approach the cabin. I stopped at the base of the stairs, breathing through my mouth. I was terrified Lloyd would throw open the door any second and train a shotgun on my face. The terror and the compulsion to know more melded into a feeling with no words to describe it. My heart hammered and a bead of sweat slid down my spine and I struggled with the urge to shake like a wet dog.

The wailing sounded again and startled me. The skin on the back of my neck prickled. It was unmistakably the girl and I couldn't be sure if she was crying out in pain or in pleasure. All I was certain of was the wail was sexual in nature. I knew I couldn't climb the steps or cross the wooden porch floor without the sound of the wooden floorboards giving me away. The flickering lights became still for the briefest moment before beginning their dance again.

I made my way slowly and quietly around to the side of the cabin. The slope of the ground made it impossible for me to look into the first window because it was above my head. But at this proximity there was the distinct and unmistakable muffled sound of flesh making contact with flesh.

I didn't want to look but knew I had to see. I had to know. I made my way to the next window at the back of the cabin. If the cabin was like mine it would have an open floor plan with only the bathroom segregated from the rest. The light emanating from the second window was dimmer than the front of the cabin. I was crouched to keep my head below the frame of the window. I couldn't hear the fleshy sounds anymore but Lloyd said something gruff and the girl moaned.

A part of me wanted to go back to my cabin and put all of this out of my head and pretend nothing was happening here and I hadn't heard anything and I hadn't had two different people inform me there was possibly something very wrong and sick happening here. But another part of me, an urgent part, guided me along. It was the same compulsion I felt when I was thirteen and Phillip was supposed to be keeping an eye on me and his girlfriend at the time, Suzy, came over and he told me to stay inside and he'd be back in a minute. I watched out the kitchen window as the two of them snuck inside the makeshift storage shed that looked more like a tree house in the backyard of the house Mom was renting at the time. I waited a few minutes before quietly sneaking out of the house and peeking in one of the grimy windows on the side of the shed and watched as the two made out. Phillip unbuttoned the girl's shirt and unfastened her bra that clipped in the front and exposed her breasts. I knew I shouldn't have intruded on my own brother but I couldn't help but stare at the girl's beasts. And once Mom's car pulled in the driveway I was forced to run inside the house and pretend I'd been in my room reading. The same thing was compelling me to see what was happening now. It wasn't breasts this time though. I could see all the breasts I wanted now with the click of a mouse. This was about confirming or abolishing gossip and rumors I'd heard and classifying them into fact or fiction categories and being done with it.

Slowly, I peeked over the window sill. The lacey curtain slightly obscured the scene within but I made out the shapes of two figures near the center of the cabin. I refocused my vision through a small hole in the lace curtain and could see what was happening more clearly. The cabin *was* an open design like mine. I was peering in through the bedroom area, which held one double bed, and the bath was on the opposite wall from where I was. The kitchen and living area were toward the front of the place and the cabin was scantily furnished. The flickering light did not come from a fireplace but from two oil lamps, one on the kitchen table and the other on the mantel of the fireplace. I couldn't be sure if there were any other light fixtures because my focus was drawn to the activity in the center of the cabin.

A chain was suspended from a beam in the center of the room with a hook on the end. The girl's hands were bound with a length of rope running from her hands to the hooked end of the chain. She was nude and facing the back of the cabin. Her long dark hair draped over her shoulders and covered her breasts. Lloyd stood a few feet behind her and from what I could decipher was also nude. The girl stood on tiptoe and arched her back to expose herself to Lloyd who I thought was fucking her with what looked like a wooden dowel rod while fondling his flaccid penis. Lloyd gave the girl's pussy a cruel thousand yard stare as he desperately tried to coax his cock into an erection. The girl let loose a wail of pleasure.

I dropped back down below the window. I squeezed my eyes tight and shook my head. I wished I hadn't seen it. Some images are burned into your brain forever no matter how much you want to forget them. Lloyd was having sex with his daughter. Point blank. Or maybe once upon a time he'd been able to have sex with her. He was unable to arouse himself now and obviously was using an aid on the girl. And from what I could divulge she appeared to be enjoying it. I'd seen too much. But everyone's assumptions were true. Whether or not Lloyd had previously had intercourse with the girl was moot. What he was doing with her right now was heinous.

A snap in the thick wall of trees at the back of the cabin drew my attention. My heart leapt into my throat. The noise was close and the sensation of something large and looming and ominous enveloped me. I thought I could detect the slightest ebb and flow of breathing coming from the same direction but it was difficult to decipher over the buzz of insects. Terror rooted me where I crouched. The presence was like a black hole or a vacuum. It welcomed you into its darkness and, for some reason unbeknownst to me, I wanted to be there. The sensation grew and faded as I imagined it moved in proximity to me. The trace of spices and ashes filled my sinuses and I fought the strong urge to sneeze. I wanted to pinch my nose or rub it but I was too frightened to move. I was certain whatever it was made its way around the back of the cabin and toward the other side, away from me. Once the smell succeeded my flight instinct kicked in.

The girl wailed again inside the cabin. I quickly and quietly retreated to my own cabin. Without a doubt there was something wrong with Lloyd and his daughter. But there was something else going on at their place besides their incestualized relationship. Both times I'd been close to their cabin I was hit with a sense of dread or sadness and the sense there was something unnatural looming over the place. Whatever it was I felt as though it manifested itself into an actual physical thing that could be detected through the senses but not seen. It was something evil and I didn't want to be anywhere near it.

12

I didn't sleep the rest of the night. I researched online how to report child abuse and found a hotline and an anonymous submission form. I chose to use the online form. My phone signal wasn't great and I didn't want the call to drop in the middle of reporting what I'd seen. I also didn't want my name associated with the report because I was terrified of Lloyd. Even reporting anonymously through the online form made me jumpy and my nerves were raw and exposed. Who else would Lloyd think reported it? There was no way he wouldn't automatically assume it was me. I was a stone's throw from it all and, from the tales I'd heard, Tryphena could've been a figment of everyone's imagination. There were very few people who even knew the girl existed.

I tried to scrub my mind of what Lloyd and Tryphena had done. And once the night was over I assumed the right authorities would fix the situation. I'd never called upon and needed the assistance of the law as an adult but I remembered the officers, a coroner, and EMS staff who came to our house when Dad died. Everyone was strong and authoritative and understanding and supportive and I couldn't see why the people who were employed with the other agency wouldn't be of the same ilk. Even more so since they dealt with children on a daily basis.

Over the next few days I resisted the urge to snoop when the sound of gravel crunching beneath tires passed in front of my cabin. I filled my time with finishing the floor and pretending my residence was the only one tucked away in the nook of trees. I filled my time with renovations to preoccupy my mind and to keep from thinking about what I'd seen and what I'd experienced outside of their cabin. It didn't seem possible for me to be disturbed by some unknown presence lingering around outside when there was an unspeakable depravity taking place within the cabin.

Sleeping on the deck now made me feel exposed and vulnerable. The feelings made it difficult for me to fall asleep soundly or get any real rest. My sense of susceptibility didn't subside much once the floor was finished and my bed was back inside either.

Moving the furniture inside without scratching the floors was challenging. But I discovered a tip online. One person suggested placing large items on blankets or towels and sliding them across the floor. Once I managed to get the furniture inside and situated I decided I deserved to take a break from physical labor for a few days before working on anything else.

I relisted my advertisements for models to reflect my new location. Phillip and I corresponded back and forth about the cabinets and he informed me he would visit in a couple of weeks to help me haul the old ones to the dumpster and bring the new ones up from the garage. I prepped for the next project by removing the cabinet doors and taking them to the dumpster since they weren't heavy and I could manage them myself.

A week after I'd listed my ad I received a secondhand message from a woman who informed me her father lost half of his foot in a farming accident several years ago. She added she'd stumbled across my advertisement and noticed it paid. She'd mentioned it to her father who was dubious of the proposition and she showed him my online gallery. He chose to relent as long as I was willing to come to his house to take the photographs. I tactfully replied to her email and told her I understood some people like the comfort of familiarity and I would be willing to travel to take the photos. We exchanged emails and agreed on a time two days later. What I didn't tell her was I was more than happy to get out of and away from my own home.

I was beginning to feel stir crazy and restless and was running out of ways to entertain myself. I found myself lying in bed, napping for a few minutes at a time. I fought the urge to stare at Lloyd's cabin in the hopes I would catch a glimpse of Child Protective Services intervening. I tossed and turned every night, fearful Lloyd would bust down my door while I slept and murder me for reporting him as a child molester. I wanted to get away from the cabin. Even if it was for only a few hours. I needed to escape the claustrophobia of the whole situation before I went mad.

The day of the shoot I packed all of my equipment into my

car and noticed nothing out of the ordinary at Lloyd's. Tryphena was not smoking on the porch and I hoped my anonymous report had done the girl good.

The photo shoot was nerve-racking. The model's name was Frank and he lived a half hour away on a large farm. He was a cantankerous old man who made snide comments about the state of my car and how an artist from the city should be able to afford a fancy vehicle. He limped around his house on a prosthetic foot and didn't seem pleased with my equipment cluttering his living room. He complained the backdrop was unnecessary. He took umbrage when I requested he remove the prosthetic and sock and allow the wear lines creasing his skin to dissipate before taking the photographs. Everything was a huge hassle to him. The daughter who'd contacted me was there. Her name was Sara and she was equally as challenging with her overly chipper attitude. She was more enthusiastic for my art than I was and was convinced the photo I used, if I used any of them, would make her father famous. I didn't take as many photos as I'd hoped. Every time I asked Frank to reposition, my request was browbeaten with complaints of the aches and pains of aging. And he ridiculed me constantly and questioned why a picture from any certain angle was needed or would be interesting.

I tried my best to take usable photos. Frank had managed to slip exiting a combine and mangle his foot when he was in his thirties. The accident severed the toes and the padded part of the foot behind the toes. The doctor's left him with the heel of his foot and a nasty scar running halfway up his shin. The whole session quickly became more awkward as I began to pack up my equipment. Sara was insistent I photograph the nearly invisible quarter inch scar on her hand. I told her I only brought enough cash to pay her father and I was suddenly thankful these people didn't know my address and for once in several days I was thankful to go home. I second guessed my thankfulness once I rounded the bend in my drive and spotted Lloyd's cabin. I preoccupied myself for the next few days by editing the photographs and did manage to salvage one decent shot.

The night before Phillip was scheduled to help me I began to feel slightly off and nauseated. I had the feeling I was getting sick and imagined it had to do with my lack of sleep. I developed a metallic taste in my mouth and tried to drown it out with orange juice and after a few hours I was convinced the juice was making the taste worse. The day felt exceptionally hot but the thermometer mounted to one of the support beams for the deck's roof read seventy-eight degrees. I began to chill while sitting outside. And once the sun was over the horizon a sensation, not a sound, started to throb in my eardrums. I tried to eat a burger for supper but my appetite was nonexistent. I sat on the deck after full darkness and suddenly all the sounds of insects and birds and small scuttling creatures came to a complete stop. There wasn't even a whisper of a rustling leaf. The silence was so complete and sudden I panicked and thought I'd experienced some illness that strikes its victims deaf instantaneously. I tested my hearing by clearing my throat and knew the abrupt loss of sound was not a physical ailment on my part. The silence was unsettling and something about it threw my equilibrium off. I was about to retrieve my laptop and research the phenomenon, chalking it up to a sign of impending bad weather, when a loud crack and crash of a tree branch in the distance startled me. The first crashing limb was followed by another, and another, and another until it sounded as though the whole forest was crashing down in the darkness.

I ran into the cabin amid the chaos and retrieved a flashlight from under the kitchen sink. The thudding of limbs hitting the soil nearby sent vibrations through the cabin and I grew worried a tree would fall on the cabin and knock in the roof. Once I had the flashlight in hand I ran back out on the deck and shone the light into the darkness, trying to make out what was happening. The light was weak and didn't penetrate far enough into the night. And as unexpectedly as it all started, the forest grew still again, and a few seconds later the sound of insects returned.

I sat in my chair on the deck, staring into the darkness and feeling stunned. I gripped the flashlight and nervously bounced my foot, waiting for something else to happen. The sound of Tryphena's wailing in the distance broke the concentration of my sentinel watch. Either my testimony wasn't enough, the organization never received it, or the two convinced the authorities nothing was happening. I shoved my index fingers in my ears like a child defiantly trying to block out another taunting child or someone telling them something they didn't want to hear. I retreated into the cabin and put on some music. I sent another message through the website describing the incident again, the previous submission, and expressed my concerns for the wellbeing of the girl. Once I was done I shut and locked all the windows and doors to blockade myself against the mental image the girl's wails provoked and went to bed early.

I woke in the middle of the night from a nightmare, sweating profusely. I removed my sweat-drenched shirt and threw it on the floor. My stomach lurched and I bolted in a sleepy and confused state to the bathroom. I barely had time to turn on the light and lift the toilet lid before I began retching. I dry heaved a few times and was only able to produce a thin stream of saliva before I felt whatever was causing the discomfort forcing itself up my esophagus. A creeping and burning sensation rose from my stomach and lodged in my throat, cutting off my ability to breathe. I heaved with no results and quickly began to panic. I couldn't draw a breath and thought I was going to die. No one was here to help me and Phillip wouldn't arrive until tomorrow and he would find me dead just like he had with Mom. And where would that leave him? I could feel the blood straining in my face as I continually tried to force the object out. I had no idea how to give myself the Heimlich and punched myself in the stomach twice. My vision was beginning to blacken around the edges when I punched my stomach a third time and the object tore free. The thing scorched my throat before landing in the toilet bowl.

I gasped for air and stared at the large prehistoric beetle with large pinchers swimming in the water. I jumped back in surprise and banged my head on the sink's countertop. I cried out in pain, rubbed my head, and slowly leaned forward to inspect the toilet's contents. I was convinced it was a trick of the eye or a hallucination brought on by a high fever. But no. There it was. The same beetle that scared me out of my sleep several nights before was trying to climb the smooth porcelain. I couldn't be sure it was the exact same beetle but it was the same species. I feared it would figure out how to fly out of the toilet and I pulled the handle to flush it away. I stared in fascination and terror as the flow of water caught the bug and it flailed as the whirlpool of water sucked it down and it disappeared.

I sat back and rubbed my battered stomach and tried to swallow. My throat burned and was dry and my Adam's apple caught when I tried to swallow and I began a hoarse coughing fit. I needed water. I made it to my feet and drank cold handfuls of water from the sink. I inspected the inside of my mouth in the mirror but was distracted by the blood seeping out of the healed scars on my chest as if they had been freshly cut again.

"What the fuck?" I rasped.

I fingered the burning incisions. My hands shook as my mind tried to process what the fuck was happening to me. I opened my mouth and inspected the red and raw back of my throat. I splashed cold water on my face and chest and cleaned myself up and racked my brain for an answer to what I'd experienced and came up with nothing other than I had to be losing my mind or experiencing fever-induced hallucinations. I reprimanded myself for not purchasing a thermometer before. It seemed like such an essential thing for a first-aid kit but having one felt like something you only kept around if you had small children. I calmed myself and tried to come up with a logical explanation to all of tonight's events and convinced myself the beetle was a figment of my imagination and I had a fever or I was sleepwalking and the branches falling in the woods were part of a fever dream. I'd never been known to sleepwalk though. At least not that I knew of. I would have to ask Phillip if he could recall a time when I experienced a bizarre set of night terrors or if I was ever a sleepwalker.

13

"You look like hell," Phillip said. "What's with the beard?"

I held the screen door for him to enter the cabin. He was dressed in the exact same worn shirt and jeans he'd worn to help me move. His face was etched with worry lines as he stepped in and looked me over. I let the spring close the screen door.

I touch the ever growing stubble on my cheek. "Figured I didn't have anyone to impress at the moment. Might as well let it grow." My throat was still sore from the night's episode and my voice hoarse. The dryness in my throat caused me to give an involuntary cough.

"You sound horrible. You should've called me before I left. We could've done this another day if you're feeling under the weather."

I waved dismissively. "It's not that bad. I sound worse than I feel." That was a lie. My throat and the cuts on my chest felt like they were being dissolved with acid. "Besides, it would've been a miracle to get a signal to call."

"You need to get a landline. They're not expensive anymore." He looked down at the floor. "I think like twenty dollars a month." His gaze followed the floorboards into the living room area.

"I have the Internet. It's good enough."

He put his hands on his hips and stared at the floor by his feet. "Floor looks good." He nodded at his own statement of approval.

"I should hope so. Do you have any idea how heavy a floor sander is? I'm surprised I didn't break my back."

"Should've asked your hillbilly neighbor for help." He laughed.

I shook my head. "Jesus . . . that guy." The image of Lloyd and Tryphena came raging back. I rubbed my temple and tried to think of anything else.

"Have you talked to him any more?"

"Not really. Thank god. The locals think they're real fucking weirdos. Says a lot since the locals are a tad off themselves."

The coffeemaker's automatic timer clicked. The coffee had been sitting on the burner for a few hours and the machine's automatic shutdown kicked in.

I said, "Want some old burned coffee?"

"My favorite."

He leaned against the kitchen counter while I prepared two mugs. We both sipped the semi-burnt brew and stared at the cupboards, assessing the situation.

I said, "The people I bought firewood from say they've never spoken to the guy in the other cabin." I didn't want to go into detail about the conversation I'd had. The thought of bringing up such a conversation with a father who had a daughter felt excessively obscene, even if he was my brother. "I was worried Mom might've had problems with him."

Phillip continued to look the cabinets over and shook his head. "She only mentioned them running the trash up for her and retrieving the mail when she got sick. She didn't tell me their names or anything. Actually, it would've been nice if they were a little more chummy with her so I wouldn't have found her . . ." He cleared his throat.

After a brief silence I said, "Sucks."

I refused to look at him. I knew the memory of trying to contact Mom and not getting a response and having to make the long drive while filled with worry only to discover Mom hadn't suddenly succumbed to the cancer she was battling but to a heart attack when we constantly insisted she needed to stay with Phillip so someone could care for her was running through his mind. She'd stubbornly refused and said once she wasn't able to take care of herself she would move in with Phillip and not a day before then would she abandon the one home she'd ever owned. It was one memory he didn't want to rehash and neither did I. I took a seat at the kitchen table. Phillip continued to stand. We both sipped our coffee.

"I've got a dumb question for you," I said.

He took a sip of his coffee and said, "What's that?"

"Did I ever sleepwalk when I was a kid?"

His face screwed up in thought. "I don't think so. Why? Have you been sleepwalking?"

"I don't know. Maybe."

"What do you mean?"

"I've been having strange dreams." I didn't want to tell him about the cuts or the beetle. I was afraid he would think I was going crazy or coming down with cabin fever or something.

"You probably need more sleep."

I nodded. "Probably."

"Well." He knocked back the last of his coffee. "We should get started if we want to get this done today."

14

I had the cabinets and countertop installed within a week and the newly freed storage beneath the cabin was nice. I decided to move the photographs and shipping supplies down there to keep the cabin from appearing cluttered. I had kept an eye on the moisture in the garage. It was surprisingly dry even after a good bout of rain.

Moving the larger prints without banging the frames on the deck was challenging. I held the last large print in front of me and stretched my neck to see around it as I made my way down the steps and into the garage. I stepped on something semi-firm as I was about to set the frame down and a loud screech startled me so bad I screamed and almost dropped the expensive frame. I instinctively stumbled backward. A shadow darted to the side of the dryer and began furiously licking its paw before looking at me indignantly. My heart hammered as the black cat returned its attention to the paw I'd most likely stepped on.

"Jesus, you scared the shit out of me."

I set the frame with the others, away from the water heater and dryer, in a corner that appeared to be the best place to keep the prints unmolested. The cat shook its paw before placing it on the ground and standing. The cat wasn't wearing a collar and didn't seem skittish. It had plenty of opportunity to bolt out the open overhead door or attack me but only stood watching me.

I squatted on my haunches and extended my hand to it. "Hey, cat. I'm sorry, buddy."

The cat took a couple of hesitant steps toward me. I cooed to it and encouraged it to come closer. It was slow going but the cat finally got close enough to smell my fingers and eventually decided to rub its face against my hand. I carefully began to stroke its head and lightly scratch behind its ears. The cat purred and rubbed its side against my leg.

"Lonely, huh?" I stood and rubbed the cat's hair from my hands. "Do you want something to eat?"

The cat stared at me and purred.

"Come on." I stepped out of the garage and turned back to see the cat who hadn't moved. I waved my hand to beckon it. "Come on. If you follow me you'll get a free meal." I made my way up the stairs and kept looking back as the cat moseyed along behind me.

I held the screen door open and tried to coax the cat inside but it stopped reluctantly a few feet from the door and sat and stared at me. I gave up after a few minutes and retreated to the kitchen. I hunted around in the cupboards until I collected two bowls and a can of tuna. I opened the tuna and dumped it into one bowl and filled the other with water.

The cat was still sitting patiently in the same spot when I returned with the two bowls. It ate the handout greedily. I sat in my chair and watched it. When the bowl was empty the cat strode toward me, and without hesitation, jumped onto my lap and curled up to sleep. I petted the creature for a few minutes before I gently moved its tail to find his furry balls.

"Just us guys out here, huh, cat?"

I let him sleep for what felt like a half hour before gently picking him up. He was groggy and let me set him in the chair to continue sleeping. I retreated down to the garage and closed the door and double checked to make sure I hadn't inherited any more creatures. The cat didn't stir when I climbed the stairs and slipped into the cabin.

I wasn't inside for more than a few minutes when my laptop emitted a soft ding—announcing I'd received an email—from its home on the coffee table. I sat on the sofa and checked the message. The email was from a woman named Rachel Lee who'd stumbled across my photographs online. She'd discovered from my website we were both located in the same state and wanted to know if I was interested in photographing her hands. She went on to describe she had polydactyly of the hands and included a picture. I opened the attachment and viewed the crude photograph with harsh lighting someone had taken for her. It was a close up of two slender hands. At first I thought the portion of the photo containing her left hand had been doctored to look like an optical illusion. But I studied it closely and counted the fingers a couple of times, touching the screen to make sure I hadn't double counted. Her left hand contained six fully formed fingers and was absent of a thumb. Her right hand contained a more common form of the abnormality. A second but smaller digit protruded from the joint of her thumb.

I responded to Rachel's email and told her I would love to photograph her. I told her we could either do the session at my place—I included my address—or if she wasn't comfortable with that arrangement I could travel to her. I attached the model release form and asked her to read it over and to ask me any questions she may have.

When I was finished sending the email I logged into my bank account to double check my balance. I had enough funds to pay Rachel for modeling but unless I sold a few photographs soon I was going to be broke. Especially if she chose for me to travel to her and I had to spend money on gas.

I stared at the computer screen and stroked my beard while contemplating a way to boost my sales. I sighed as I logged onto the site I operated my store through and spent an hour figuring out how to make a discount code. Once I successfully generated a code giving the customer twenty percent off their purchase I visited the two social networking sites I rarely had anything to do with. I tried to recall the last time I visited either site and was certain it was when I still lived with Naomi. Interacting through email was my preferred method of communicating with customers and models. I didn't like the format of social networking and the empty throwaway conversations and time suck it created. But Naomi suggested I try to use it as a free platform to advertise my photography. I reluctantly signed up for two of the major social networking sites but didn't have much success in creating fans because I had no idea where to start or what to do. Taking a photograph and capturing what someone would want to study . . . I knew how to do that. Rallying people to fawn over said photos? That was a crapshoot. You had to know the right people. Or know the right indirect line of people. You had to strike the fancy of one person who would talk to a certain friend and then their friend would talk to another person, maybe a coworker, who would relay the right amount of enthusiasm to the next person and so on and so forth until it reached the one specific person who could pull the right strings and shove you into the dim limelight for your fifteen seconds of mediocre fame. And once it was over and you fell back into the nobody category you would be lucky if in six months someone you'd never met had a conversation with a friend and said 'whatever happened to *that* guy'. I knew art was in its death throes but I still refused to admit it aloud and I was going to fight it until I was forced to take up what Naomi referred to as 'a real job'.

The first site I logged onto was sad. There weren't any notifications from the few followers I'd obtained when I first opened the account. I went ahead and constructed a post announcing the sale and providing the code. I knew it wouldn't generate much interest but I was hopeful maybe I could eke out one sale even though I never interacted with anyone.

Once I was finished I moved onto the other site. I was surprised to find a dozen friend requests and even more surprised one was from a Rachel Lee. I clicked on her profile and looked at the self-taken photograph of an extremely pretty woman with tawny shoulder-length hair and gray eyes. Her profile information indicated she lived in the same location as the Rachel

Lee who'd emailed me. It also informed me she was a painter and a sometime singer and she was twenty-five. I still wasn't convinced it was the same Rachel who'd contacted me about having her photograph taken so I began scrolling through her scant amount of photos, none revealing her hands, until I discovered a photograph of her in a bikini lying on a beach towel with a couple of other women near her age. She was laughing and holding her one hand up in a manner suggesting she wanted to take the camera away from the photographer. And there in the photograph was the unmistakable double thumb. Her other hand was on her towel and hidden by one of the other women's hips. I stared at the hand briefly but I couldn't help but ogle what the photograph revealed. Rachel was attractive. And the more I stared at the photo the more I became aroused by the smooth curves and soft lines of her lightly tanned flesh.

Under normal circumstances I wasn't an uncontrollable deviant who masturbated to family photos of women enjoying a vacation on the beach. But I was lonely. Sexual release was maintenance to keep me sane and keep me from becoming an insufferable and cranky cunt when I did interact with people. The thought of such an attractive girl even acknowledging I existed sparked sexual feelings within me that wouldn't be quenched or fulfilled until I followed through. With no shame I unfastened my pants and pushed them and my underwear down just far enough to expose my fully erect cock. I pulled up my shirt, lubed my hand with some precome, and began to masturbate. I stared at the shadowed skin of Rachel's cleavage as I stroked my penis and tried to imagine what her nipples would look like and envisioned her with a hairless pink pussy. I closed my eyes and conjured an image of Rachel masturbating with her left hand and sliding her six fingers over her wet cunt and slipping a couple of her fingers inside her pussy right before I came on my lower stomach.

I pulled my shirt off and used it to clean myself before tucking my cock back into my underwear and refastening my pants. I closed the photo of Rachel and accepted her friend request along with the other requests. I proceeded to construct a post about the sale and added it to the stream of social media. I sat the laptop on the coffee table and proceeded to throw my shirt in the dirty clothes and wash my hands.

The computer dinged again and I checked it. It was a response email from Rachel. She informed me she had always wanted to visit the area where I lived and check out the park and was willing to drive to my place for the photos. She asked if I was available the upcoming weekend. I replied to her email and told her I was available and any time she chose was fine. I included my address and gave some helpful landmark indicators to help her and sent the email. I had another browser window still open to the social networking site and noticed a notification had appeared. I clicked on it and realized Rachel had shared my post about the sale and gleefully boasted she was going to have her photo taken by me. My computer made a queer noise and a small window popped up in the lower right hand corner of my screen. It was a chat box from the social networking site and it was a message from Rachel. She asked if noon on Saturday was fine and she followed it with a second brief message apologizing for using the chat format but she stated it was quicker than sending an email thread back and forth. I typed noon on Saturday was fine and hit send. Three bouncing dots appeared and disappeared and then the word 'cool' appeared. The bouncing dots came and went and another message took their place asking if it was okay she had shared my post. I carefully typed I appreciated the share and hoped it generated a sale. A smiley face appeared in the chat box, sent from Rachel. I waited for another response or bouncing dots. Nothing happened. I wasn't sure if I should respond with a goodbye but after a length of time passed I was certain no response was needed.

My attention was distracted from Rachel when the email indicator sounded. I found an email for an order in my inbox. I retreated outside to retrieve the photograph and shipping materials. The cat looked up at me when I opened the door. He had made himself comfortable in my chair. I knew I should probably buy a bag of cat food when I dropped the photograph off at the post office. And I wondered if Rachel liked cats.

15

Time dragged the few days leading up to Rachel's scheduled shoot. I became excited and nervous and filled with an anticipation I hadn't experienced since I first started dating Naomi. At first I ignored it, and even though there was no one around to witness it, I tried to remain cool and calm and told myself it was a business affair and I had to remain neutral and professional. But I recognized the feeling of wanting and desire as soon as I closed my laptop after the chat with Rachel. But I didn't admit it to myself until the next day when I shaved my beard off. My face felt exposed and sensitive afterward and I recognized my soul and emotional wellbeing were in the same state. I tried to tell myself Rachel already had a boyfriend, even though there was no information in her relationship status, and was too pretty and smart to be interested in dating a deadbeat photographer. She would come, have her photo taken, and vanish into the unattainable monster of life and time and never be seen or heard from on my end ever again.

I nitpicked things around the cabin. I cleaned the place daily and became even more finicky when the cat decided he wanted to follow me inside after I fed him some cat food. I designated an extra throw pillow from the sofa as his bed and threw it on the floor. I picked him up and sat him on the pillow. He kneaded it with his front paws immediately and eventually curled up on it. I didn't want him on the sofa or bed because I had an irrational fear Rachel might be allergic to cats. He would paw at the door when he wanted out and luckily didn't decide to mark the cabin as his own by urinating on the floor. The screen door to the deck was spring loaded and never latched properly without giving the door a firm push against the frame. The cat quickly figured out he could let himself out by pushing on the door, which I left unlatched most of the time, but a couple of hours later he would return and yowl until I let him in.

I was keyed up and anxious and slept fitfully each night even after having a couple of beers as a sleep aid. The night before Rachel's photo shoot I dreamed an unseen force beckoned me into an unknown darkness. I couldn't see anything in the dream and an unknown energy whispered things to me and told me it had knowledge of my destiny and said I was part of a bigger plan and it needed me.

The sentence it spoke was delivered menacingly. It said, "Everything will be fine if you just let me in." The thing then tried to shove its large, clawed hands down my throat.

I awoke to find myself lying on my back on the cool forest floor, naked. The sun had barely risen and the trees were looming gray shadows in the civil twilight. The confusion of waking up in a strange place without clothes set me into a panic. I sat up and found the cat sitting a few feet from me by a cluster of small trees, staring at me.

I stood and said, "What the hell, cat?" I looked around, hoping I was within eyeshot of the cabin but all I could see were trees. I looked down at my naked flesh and felt my damp skin in some ridiculous gesture as if I were checking to make sure *I* was real.

I turned back to the cat. What I originally thought was a cluster of trees the cat sat beside was something entirely different. Each of the tree trunks was approximately two to three inches in diameter. The trees were interwoven with each other and twisted at such severe angles it was impossible the thing could have grown into the design naturally. The base of the first cluster of trees formed the first enormous foot and continued into a well-muscled calf and thigh. A short distance from the first foot there was another foot comprised of the same type of gnarled and twisted trees. The two legs connected and formed a muscular torso with two elongated arms. The fingers were made of thorny branches and nearly twelve inches in length. The head was elongated and misshapen and whoever constructed the thing had managed to render the thin branches into a terrifying expression on the thing. The whole thing stood close to eight feet tall. I was equally frightened and intrigued by it. If I had my camera I would've taken several photos.

The cat stood and began to trot off. I had no idea where he was headed but all I could do was follow him and hope he would lead me home. I had to jog to keep up with the cat, which proved to be difficult without shoes. I kept my hand over my penis. I had no idea where I was or how close I was to any hiking trails. The last thing I wanted was to be arrested for indecent exposure. I grew winded as I tried to keep up with the cat and scraped the bottom of my foot on something sharp. I ignored the pain and tried not to think about the possibility of having an open cut on the bottom of my foot and the wound was getting packed full of dirt and leaves and whatever other debris lay on the forest floor. The sky lightened as I struggled to keep up with the cat. After what felt like an hour I was exhausted and sweaty and breathing heavily and had developed a stitch in my side. I finally spotted a break in the trees. I recognized my cabin and slowed down to catch my breath and walked the rest of the way, careful not to step on anything that would damage my feet further.

As I approached the cabin I tried to comprehend what had happened. There was no other explanation than sleepwalking. It was disturbing. Phillip said he couldn't remember me sleepwalking when I was a kid. And Naomi never mentioned it. But even if I was sleepwalking how had I made it that far into the woods in complete darkness without a scrape? It had been difficult enough with scant morning light. But in complete darkness? There wasn't a mark on me other than one on my foot which I managed to pick up this morning on my way home. And how did I know to go to that exact location? It didn't seem plausible I happened to stop a few feet from the one random spot in the enormous and vast forest where someone had taken it upon themselves to construct a demented effigy out of growing trees.

I shook all the thoughts from my head once I reached the

stairs of the cabin. I probably needed to visit a doctor. And I would've called a doctor and set up an appointment immediately if I had insurance. Just another perk of living the artist life. Health roulette. Cross your fingers and pray you never get sick or you get the privilege of paying thousands of dollars you don't have in hospital bills or taken to small claims court. I debated whether what I was experiencing was worth the debt. What I was experiencing wasn't life-threatening. I was certain I would end up in an institution or told it was a psychosomatic symptom of stress if I visited a doctor. Especially once they found out my family history. Neither diagnosis was desirable nor affordable and I decided unless I became terrified I might die or hurt someone else I could handle myself.

The cat stood outside the door and yowled at me once I reached him. He bolted inside and up to his bowl, meowing indignantly, as I checked my foot. There was a scratch on the sole of my foot but the wound barely broke the skin and had already stopped bleeding. The shirt and underwear I had worn to bed were piled on the floor by the sofa. When I stooped to retrieve them I noticed the unmistakable stain of dried semen on the shirt. *What the hell had happened last night?* The cat interrupted my thought by yowling louder. I gave him some food and checked the time. I had two hours to eat, shower, and set up my equipment for Rachel. I set out to do those things as quickly as possible. The cabin was stuffy and I started by turning on the ceiling fans and opening the doors and windows. When I opened the front door I decided I might need to add another type of lock to keep me from wandering outside at night.

I turned on some music but kept the volume low. There was

the sound of tires on the gravel drive a few minutes after noon as I fidgeted with an umbrella light stand. I resisted the urge to climb the stairs and meet her after I heard a car door shut. I kept pretending to mess with the camera equipment as I caught the sound of her descending the last of the steps.

She rapped lightly on the screen door and in a soft singsong voice said, "Hello."

I set down my camera and opened the door for her. She wore a cheerful expression and was every bit as pretty as her online photos. She wore a casual pair of cut off jean shorts to exhibit her toned and slightly tanned legs and a blue tank top with sneakers. Her tank top battled with the gray of her eyes and made them appear bluer than what they actually were.

"Rachel?" I said. Without thinking, I extended my hand to shake.

Her cheerfulness wavered for the briefest second before she extended her hand and took mine. "Yes," she responded.

Once her double thumb crossed over the top of my hand I realized my faux pas. Her hands obviously made her self-conscious and I felt like the biggest tool alive. I wasn't sure what to say. I wanted to apologize but pointing out my blunder seemed like it would only make the situation worse. My chagrin must have been prominent on my face when I let go of her hand.

She gave a small laugh. "It's okay. It happens a lot. I'm more used to the other person reacting badly, though. You know? Verbally pointing it out so other people around will stare or start asking bizarre questions. It makes me reluctant to shake hands with people." She tucked her left hand in the back pocket of her shorts.

I said, "Sorry. I didn't mean to make you uncomfortable. Habit."

She nodded and said lightheartedly, "No problem."

A breeze drifted through the screen door and touched both of us. She smelled like cedar and my cock began to stiffen. I thought about the items I needed to get at the store and the odd wooden effigy in the woods and tried to will my growing erection away.

"I'm nervous," I said. I didn't know why I was compelled to share that tidbit of information with her.

She gave me a queer look. "Nervous?"

I motioned to the black backdrop I'd set up against the living room area wall to change the subject. "We'll be shooting over here."

She took a couple of steps toward the backdrop. I quickly double checked my untucked T-shirt to make sure it was long enough to cover my erection. Rachel slipped off her shoes before stepping onto the non-reflective material suspended from the support stand and spread out across the floor.

She turned to me and said, "How do you want me?"

I knew she was asking about positioning for the photo but my hard cock played a scene in my head where I responded with 'any way you want' before I pounced on her and we both ripped off each other's clothes and pulled each other's hair and fucked and sucked and bit and spanked and fucked and fucked and fucked until we were both raw and exhausted. Once my mind hit the gutter it was like watching a drunken hobo trying to climb back out.

I said, "Um . . ." I assessed the situation. "Maybe you could kneel and lay your forearms flat on the floor."

I retrieved a pillow from the sofa and dropped it on the floor for her to kneel on. I suppressed a groan when the image of her kneeling on the pillow to suck my cock flashed through my mind.

"Oh," she said and retrieved a folded piece of paper from her pocket and handed it to me. "The model consent."

I took the paper from her and slipped it into my own back pocket. She knelt on the pillow and extended her arms on the backdrop, palms down. She appeared to be praying or throwing herself down to beg for mercy from a more powerful being. She lifted her head and observed me as I repositioned the lights around her.

"Let me know if you need a break," I said. "Or if you feel un-comfortable."

"I'm okay."

I took up the camera and stood over her. I snapped a few photos of just her hands and then some of her forearms and hands. I had her flip her hands palm up and repeated the set. Then I asked her to grab the wrist of her left arm but she hid the double thumb under her wrist.

I said, "Is it okay if I reposition your hand?"

She laughed and I gave her a questioning glance.

"You're asking permission to touch me?" She laughed again.

"I don't want to make you uncomfortable. It's just the two of us here and—"

"You can touch me."

Her response, combined with the hint of amusement in her eyes, stirred a want for her so strong it made me ache from my throat to my balls. My nervousness reached a peak and a prickle of sweat formed on my back. I squatted and my jeans pulled tightly against my painfully erect penis. I wished with everything within my soul this beautiful girl didn't happen to notice my hard penis and deem me a deviant who had no control over his body and created an awkward situation. Or that I was some crazy deformity or birth defect sex fetishist. My hand trembled as I gently repositioned her double thumb to lie naturally on top of her wrist as her other fingers wrapped around.

She said, "What song is this?"

"Huh?" I listened to the music coming from my laptop. It was one of many throwaway ambient tracks I played in the background while I worked. "Oh . . . um. I play this stuff all the time. I can change it if you like."

"No, I like it."

"I'm terrible with names. I use a streaming site and build playlists. I hardly pay attention to band names anymore. Guess that makes me sound old, huh?"

"You're not old. How old are you?"

"Thirty." I stood and looked at the laptop screen and told her the name of the band.

"If you're old that means I'm five years from being old."

I smiled at her and returned to my position. I focused the camera on her hands. I took another round of photos. We spent the next fifteen minutes exchanging our likes and dislikes in music and movies and found we were both interested in a lot of the same things and we both made recommendations of things the other hadn't heard or seen. It felt surreal to know there was at least one extraordinarily beautiful woman out there I had a lot in common with. Naomi didn't care for my music and acted as though I were torturing her when I took her to a movie I was interested in. We didn't have much in common in the way of entertainment or hobbies. She was more into mainstream things and I preferred stuff off the beaten path. But we had been of the same mindset and temperament and it was enough for us to coincide for seven years. My nervousness subsided some as I got the vague feeling Rachel was flirting with me. I considered it wishful thinking and she was trying to be courteous. But when she finally asked the one question that would drop her into vaguely interested I double checked myself.

"So," she said. "Do you live here with your girlfriend?"

"No. I live here alone." My hands began to tremble again and I snapped the last few photos I wanted. I checked the last photo I'd taken on the LCD screen of my camera to make sure it wasn't completely blurred from my unsteady hands. "I think I got all the pictures I need. You can stand up."

She stood and hobbled a couple of steps. "My feet are asleep." She laughed and took a seat on the sofa.

The cat yowled at me through the back screen door to be let in.

I said, "You're not allergic to cats, are you?"

"No. I love cats. My landlord doesn't allow pets but I'd love to have a furry companion someday."

I strode to the door with my camera in hand and said, "He won't be quiet until I let him in."

I pushed the screen door open and the cat hurried in but stopped short when it noticed Rachel. She cooed to him and extended her hand toward him. He approached her cautiously but quickly took to rubbing up against her leg as she petted him.

"What's its name?" she said.

I shrugged. "I haven't given him one. I call him Cat."

"You don't have a name?" she talked to the cat in a soft voice and petted him.

I carefully laid my camera on the bed and briefly wished I was laying Rachel on the bed. I hadn't felt this much desire for a girl since the hormonal days of high school and I began to think I was turning into an old pervert who couldn't be in the company of a pretty girl without sporting a raging hard on. I also hadn't had sex besides masturbation in a few months. I discretely readjusted my hard cock and retrieved my wallet off the top of the dresser. I counted out the bills and tried to hand her the money. She shook her head at me. I gave her a confused look and shook my money welding arm slightly to reaffirm she should take the cash.

"I feel bad taking your money," she said. "I didn't really do anything."

"I insist. It's a modeling royalty. I'm going to sell your photo to make money for myself. It wouldn't be fair if you weren't compensated."

She rubbed her hands together to rid them of cat hair and took the money reluctantly. She was tucking it in her back pocket when a knock on the front screen door startled the both of us and the cat. The cat sprinted to the back door and let himself out. Rachel appeared surprised and amused by the cat's ability to open the door.

I headed for the front door. I did a double take and stumbled over my feet when I realized the visitor was Tryphena. A million thoughts and questions raced through my mind all at once. Hadn't Child Services removed her from her home? If the authorities knew what happened why was she back in Lloyd's custody? Why was she here? Was Lloyd hidden beyond my line of sight and ready to beat me to a pulp for reporting him? But ultimately, was she in trouble and seeking refuge from her father? Her presence gave off a vibe of danger and set my heart into a sprint.

I stopped a few feet from the door. "Tryphena?"

In my peripheral Rachel leaned her head to see who was at the door. Without invitation, Tryphena opened the screen door and stepped inside. The girl wore a low cut spaghetti strap tank top that might have been a size or two too small for her breasts. The tank top was cut in such a way that if she moved wrong I was certain her nipples would be exposed and it made me uneasy. She also wore shorts entirely too short for a girl her age and sandals. Her skin appeared flush from the sun and it made the thick white scar across her neck stand out even more. It didn't seem possible for such a young girl to possess the petty intellect to produce a cruel and conniving smile, but it was the expression she currently wore.

"What are you doing here?" I said in a tone that could be deemed both surprised and accusatory. I forced myself to sound more authoritative and concerned. "Is everything okay?"

She said, "You said I could see your photos sometime." She tucked her hands into her pockets and bent one leg behind her and tapped the toe of her sandal on the floor.

She appeared to be pulling some innocent girl act in comparison to how she acted the time we spoke on her porch. I'd forgotten about my previous offer. And I regretted it when I proposed the idea but now I downright loathed myself for ever speaking to the girl.

Rachel waved from the sofa and said, "Hello."

Tryphena's attention snapped to Rachel and her expression shifted for the briefest second to one I could only describe as a snarl. The compulsion to slap Tryphena came out of nowhere and surprised me. I was not a physically violent person. I'd never struck a woman or had a desire to until that very moment. The idea of hitting a woman sickened me, especially one underage, and I wasn't sure where the thought came from and it frightened me. Rachel induced a strange feeling within me and it resounded as something protective. And the nasty and hateful expression Tryphena shot her played with a strong gut reaction to defend Rachel viciously.

I took a few steps toward Rachel and waved my hand between the two to insinuate the other. "Rachel, this is Tryphena, my neighbor's daughter and, Tryphena, this is Rachel. I just finished taking a set of photos of Rachel."

Rachel said, "Hi."

I said, "I promised Tryphena she could look at my photos sometime."

"Oh," Rachel said. "That sounds fun." She took on the tone an adult uses when speaking to a child and looked to the girl for a response.

Tryphena greeted her with an unwelcoming silence. A few seconds ticked by and with each passing second the whole situation grew excruciatingly awkward on account of Tryphena's icy demeanor.

Rachel's eyes bounced between the girl and me. "Well," she said. She slapped her thighs lightly before standing. "I should get going."

My first instinct was to beg her to stay but I didn't want to appear desperate and knew Tryphena's presence would only sour the mood we'd playfully built. With each step Rachel took toward the door I felt an opportunity slipping through my fingers and knew I had to at least try and ask her out or I would regret it.

"I'll walk you to your car," I said and immediately added, "I'll be right back," in Tryphena's direction to indicate she shouldn't follow us.

I followed Rachel up the stairs and couldn't stop from staring at her buttocks. I wanted to pull her back against my chest and run my hand up the leg of her shorts and stroke the tender soft skin where her buttock met her thigh, just a few inches from her pussy, and breathe in her scent and wait for her body heat to increase as her desire to be fucked and to come began to build. I should've masturbated before Rachel arrived. But time had been limited once I made it home and my thoughts had been too wrapped up in what had happened for me to wander so far from home and not remember any of it. I was horny and I couldn't stop staring at Rachel's ass and I knew once she was gone the unreleased sexual tension would transition me into a grumpy beast until I jerked off. All I wanted was release and I would have to deal with Tryphena and find a way to run her off so I could masturbate. Realizing my state of agitation made me realize my horniness also played into why I'd thought of slapping Tryphena before.

Rachel had parked in the parking space far enough to one side to allow her to open her door fully. She turned to me once she opened the driver's door of her newer Toyota. We both spoke at the same time. She said, "I enjoyed coming out—" I said, "I appreciate you allowing me—" We both chuckled. She watched me and mindlessly played with her car keys.

I finished my sentence. "I really appreciate you allowing me to take your photo."

She said, "I had fun." After a second she added, "I wouldn't mind hanging out again if you're not too busy."

"No," I said a little too enthusiastically. "I'm free most of the time."

"I'm staying in the area for a couple of days. I'd heard of the park before and figured I'd turn the trip here into a mini vacation and check out some of the waterfalls. If you're not busy tomorrow you could join me . . . unless hiking isn't your thing."

"That sounds wonderful."

"Great! I can pick you up at noon?"

"Sure."

She fidgeted and appeared pensive for a second. I extended my hand again for a shake. She gave me a clumsy hug so quickly I didn't have time to process what she was doing or have time to return the gesture before she let go. She hopped in her car and started it.

She rolled down her window and said, "See you tomorrow."

I stepped out of the way so she could back up and waved at her. She backed out of the parking space and returned my wave before taking off down the drive. She tapped her horn before taking the turn toward onto the incline.

I got the sense the attraction between the two of us was mutual or at the very least I may have managed to pique her interest for a couple of days. The idea of such a beautiful woman wanting anything to do with me felt unreal and made me giddy. I turned to head back inside and spotted Lloyd's cabin and felt all the pent up joy draining from my body.

The screen door of Lloyd's cabin was dark and the station wagon was gone. A state of panic set in when I realized Lloyd wasn't aware his daughter was in my cabin. There was an urgency to placate Tryphena by showing her the photos—pictures with content that could possibly make her take umbrage with me—as quickly as possible and get her out of my house.

I wanted to know if the correct personnel had become involved with her and Lloyd's situation and, if they had investigated the two, why she was still living with him. But I also didn't want to become involved. If the authorities hadn't been to their house yet I didn't want to tip them off I knew what was happening and the law was probably going to be involved soon.

16

I was perplexed by my persistent hard on and did my damnedest to will it away as I descended the stairs to the cabin. It was difficult to think of anything other than Rachel and the thousands of different possibilities and scenarios tomorrow could potentially bring.

My mind cleared quickly of Rachel and filled with anxiety when I entered the cabin and found Tryphena fondling my camera by the bed. There was something about the girl that filled me with a foreboding sense of dread every time I saw her. It was as if guile oozed from her pores and I sensed whatever she was conniving to do would destroy whoever got caught up in her crosshairs.

"Please don't touch that," I said a tad too abrasively.

"Okay," she said.

She gave me a snarky smile and held the camera out to me in a haphazardly fashion. I had a glimpse of her dropping the camera on purpose and it shattering into a million unfixable pieces on the floor. I crossed the cabin and took the camera from her.

"Sorry," I said and set the camera on the dresser. "It's an expensive piece of equipment and my livelihood. I can't afford for anything to happen to it."

Tryphena ignored my concern for the camera's safety and looked around the cabin. She said, "Where are the photos?"

"I keep them in the garage."

She lifted her hands to clear a strand of her long hair from her face. She gathered her hair into a ponytail and pulled it off the back of her neck briefly before letting it all fall down her back, making the scar on her neck more visible. Her nipples threatened to slip free of her tank top when she lifted her arms. I turned my attention to the backdrop and tried to think of anything other than my engorged cock and its unyielding nagging to be released.

"Can I see them?" she said.

I wanted to tell her no. I wanted to tell her maybe she should come back with her father. But I knew Lloyd frightened and chilled me to the bone in a way that made me never want to be within eyesight of the man ever again. I didn't want him in my house any more than I wanted Tryphena here at the moment. How was I going to explain the photos to her? Should I explain them at all or let her interpret them for herself? Her presence made me extremely uncomfortable and even more so in my continuous and unyielding state of arousal. She was a budding young woman busting out of her clothes and I was a horny tricenarian who would've sworn up to this moment my morals were more impeccable than the deplorable thoughts racing through my brain.

"Sure," I said, "you can look. Well . . . maybe not all of them. Some of the photos have—"

"Nudity?" She raised her eyebrows.

"Uh, yes. So is the nature of art." I rubbed the back of my neck nervously. "And you're underage."

She waved her hand dismissively. "It's not like I haven't seen a cock before."

The nonchalant way she said the word 'cock' was pornographic and filthy coming from such a young girl's mouth. Her uncouth language sparked something within me and became the big sparkling bow on a package labeled taboo.

"I don't want to piss off your dad."

With a touch of salaciousness she said, "He doesn't have to know. There are a lot of things about me he doesn't know."

I ignored whatever it was she was implying and agreed she could see the photos. She followed me out of the cabin and down the stairs to the garage. I decided the best course of action was to allow her to hurriedly take a look and then tell her I had an appointment or a phone call to make to get her to leave before her father came home. And then I could have some time to myself to think about Rachel and to liberate myself of all the pent up sexual energy.

I stopped before opening the door and said, "Before you see them I need to explain the subject matter." I paused and avoided looking directly at her scar. "I specialize in taking photos of human malformations, amputations, deformities, and . . ." I was reluctant to say the last word. "Scars."

There was a nearly imperceptible drop in her demeanor.

"Cool!" she said with a false enthusiasm.

"Are you sure?"

"You promised I could see them. Stop stalling."

I nodded, opened the overhead door, and turned on the light. I leaned against the dryer as she approached the framed photos stacked carefully against the wall. The photos weren't shamed the way they were at Phillip's and they were facing out. She ran her fingers along the frame containing a photo of a man with two child-sized legs and one malformed arm of his parasitic twin protruding from his chest. The photo was in black and white and the shot was of the man's naked torso and face. Normally I didn't include the model's face but the man's expression struck me as an important inclusion when I began editing. The subject stared at the viewer with a haunted expression. Tryphena stared at the photograph for a few seconds before tipping the frame forward to view the one behind it.

She slowly shuffled through my inventory—taking time to process and observe each one—with a neutral expression. I stood by anxiously, afraid she might damage a frame, and listened carefully for the sound of Lloyd returning. A shadow moved in my peripheral. I turned my attention to the trees and spotted the cat. He eyed the two of us dubiously and skittered along the tree line before disappearing around the side of the cabin. There was a sudden shift in air pressure that caused my ears to ring and for a few seconds it was all I could hear. I pushed the tender indentation behind one of my ears with my index finger and opened and closed my jaw, trying to relieve the discomfort. Vertigo hit me for a brief moment and I got an overwhelming sensation I was being watched. I scanned the trees for any movement and my hearing finally returned.

"I like them," Tryphena said.

I turned my attention back to her. She stood with her hands tucked into her back pockets, facing me.

"Thank you," I said.

She took a few steps toward me. "Do you want to take my picture?"

"Excuse me?"

"Oh, come on." She removed one hand from her pocket and touched the scar on her neck. "Isn't this why you invited me down here?"

I tried to come up with a sensible excuse. It was true. Originally, upon meeting them, I did want to take her and Lloyd's photo. But I'd always been sensitive to people who struck me as odd and I viewed craziness and catastrophe as highly contagious diseases and the two of them seemed to be constructed of the stuff. The more you tried to help someone who was out of control or in need of help, and the more you allowed them into your life, the more likely you would be sucked into whatever madness they viewed as normal.

"No," I responded. "You seemed interested in photography when we spoke and I thought you might be interested in them."

An unruly strand of her hair fell in her face and she flipped her head to shake it away. She took a couple more steps toward me. She stopped a foot in front of me and tilted her head slightly to make the scar more prominent. Her proximity made me uncomfortable and overtly aware I was still aroused. The amount of naked flesh forming her cleavage, but barely stopping short of exposing her nipples, was distracting.

"Touch it," she said.

Her command confused me. "No. That's okay."

"You want to know the story behind it?"

"I don't ask. If the model wants to tell me, I listen. But I never prompt the subject. Sometimes the emotional scars are deeper than the physical ones."

She gave a dry chuckle. "Your photos kinda show there's beauty in tragedy, you know?"

I nodded.

"But I don't think you get the people," she said. "You don't feel their pain. *You* don't have any scars."

Her statement angered me. "I have plenty of scars. I'm not perfect. No one is," I snapped. My thoughts flashed to the scarred symbol on my chest. "Like I said, not everyone's scars are visible. Some people are more damaged on the inside than anything I've photographed." I flicked my wrist at the pictures to insinuate them.

"Do you ever get the feeling some people hurt themselves to feel something . . . or to feed something bigger than their own selfish misery?"

"Is that what you did?" I nodded toward her neck.

She smiled coyly at me but didn't respond.

"You're a strange kid. I think you should probably head back home."

"I'm not a kid," she said angrily. She quickly regained her smile. "Do you want to take my photo?"

"You already asked me that. You're underage. I would need your dad to sign a consent form."

"Age is a number."

She laid her hand on my hard on and rubbed it through the material of my jeans. I grabbed her wrist roughly, twisted it, and pulled her hand away. She gasped and looked equal parts shocked and amused.

"What the fuck are you doing?!"

I held her wrist too tightly and it felt thin and fragile, as though it might break were I to apply any more pressure..

"Come on," she said. "You've had a boner since I arrived. I know you want me." Lightning fast, she slipped her other hand under the bottom of my shirt and unfastened my jeans.

I grabbed her other wrist and yanked it away before she could do anything further. While holding both of her wrists I gave her a small shove, not wanting to hurt her. She stumbled back a couple of steps. I refastened my pants.

"I think it's time for you to leave," I said.

She stared at me incredulously.

"Now," I said.

She gave me a furious stare before she pounced on me. She rubbed her body against mine and I fell back against the dryer. She grabbed the back of my neck and tried to pull me into a kiss. I leaned away from her and tried to push her away but she clung to me like glue. She stood on her tiptoes and hopped up and tried to plant her mouth on mine. Her other hand slid down my pants and she began to stroke my cock.

I shouted, "Stop it! Get off me!"

She let go of the back of my neck but kept all of her weight on me and still held my dick. She said, "I'm so fucking horny. Give me what I want and I won't tell my papa you raped me."

"What!? I'm not raping you! Let go!"

I grabbed at her wrist to pull her hand off my cock. She gripped my penis hard and grabbed my balls through the material of my pants with her other hand. She gave my balls a firm squeeze and a pain shot into my stomach. The sensation made me feel like I needed to either vomit or take a shit. I was bent backward over the dryer as she pressed against me. Her face was inches from mine and I could smell some type of sweet gum or candy mixed with cigarette smoke on her breath.

She said, "I'll tell him you did something worse."

"That's blackmail. I'll go to jail for statutory rape."

"I'm old enough to make my own decisions."

She let go of my balls and eased her grip from my cock. I was desperately trying to will away the erection and thought the pain would have staunched it but my body was having nothing to do with rationality. She pushed off of me slightly and moved her hand from my cock to unfasten and unzip my pants. I noticed during our struggle her nipples had finally sprung free from her tank top and suddenly all of my attempts to go limp were in vain. She quickly pulled my underwear and pants down. She lowered her head, pulled her hair over one shoulder, held the top my cock in one hand, and ran her tongue slowly from my balls to the tip of my dick, glistening with precome. She kept her eyes locked on mine through the whole act.

I groaned, "I'm going to burn in hell."

"Be quiet," she whispered.

She took the tip of my cock in her mouth and stroked me slowly a couple of times, her eyes never leaving mine. I shut my eyes and could feel something sacred and unreplaceable within me shatter. I tried to think of anything else than what was happening. I tried to conjure vile images to force myself to go soft. After a minute of her slowly manipulating me her warm mouth and hand left my dick. I realized how sore my back was from being bent backward. I opened my eyes and stood up straight and hoped what had happened was all she wanted. Instead she pulled her tank top down to her waist and slipped out of her sandals simultaneously. She unbuttoned her shorts and pushed all of her clothing down her legs in one fluid motion and stacked her clothes on top of the sandals. She had a small and sparse patch of pubic hair.

I groaned again and began to reach for my pants and under-wear but she chastised me and warned me again to do what she wanted or face jail. She kicked the pile of clothes closer to me before dropping to her knees, using her discarded clothing as a cushion. She placed her hands on my hips and took my whole cock into her mouth slowly and gagged when the tip of my dick touched the back of her throat. The spasm in her throat caused the back of her tongue to bounce against the sensitive part on the underside of the head and the urge to thrust was strong. She wrapped her lips over her teeth and began to slowly give me head. I felt the orgasm build quickly.

I gripped the top of the dryer behind me and said, "If you don't stop I'm going to come."

She hummed an agreeable sound and sped up.

I reached forward to grab the back of her head but rethought my action. I didn't know if she would have an issue with me holding her head. Naomi didn't mind it but some women hated it. And I definitely didn't want to do anything that could be construed as me forcing myself on this girl. I wasn't going to last much longer. It had been so long since I'd felt the heat of another person during sex and my brain was screaming at me I was going to burn in hell and it was taboo and exciting and new and I was suddenly reminded of being sixteen and losing my virginity to a girl I dated briefly one summer named Jennifer who'd already lost her virginity and during the initial act I'd gotten so fucking nervous I lost my hard on and she blamed herself and questioned her appeal to me and I tried to explain to her it wasn't her as she tried to prime my soft penis into something fuckable. Our second attempt was more successful.

I was pulled from my reverie by the building orgasm. I grabbed Trypena's shoulder and said, "I'm going to come."

She hummed another agreeable sound and continued.

With a sense of urgency I tapped her shoulder. "I'm going to come in your mouth."

Again, the agreeable sound.

"All right."

My body tensed as I orgasmed hard. The sensation ran deep into my belly and I held the dryer to keep from falling. Tryphena continued to suck me as my orgasm subsided. She pulled her mouth from my cock, sucking and flicking her tongue on the underside as she did so. She sucked on the extra sensitive tip, nearly causing me pain, before removing her mouth and swallowing my come. She giggled and wiped her mouth with the back of her hand. I quickly pulled my pants up, tucked my softening cock back into my underwear, and refastened my pants.

With my pent up sexual energy drained I was filled with guilt and panic and nauseated and near the brink of tears. I wanted the girl to leave but I'd somehow become mute when I tried to open my mouth to speak. I felt like vomiting.

Tryphena stood and hopped up on the washer. She situated herself so she was sitting on the edge, spread her legs, and began fingering herself. "Time to return the favor," she said. She removed her glistening fingers from her pussy and sucked on them. With her free hand she pinched the nipple of one of her breasts. She removed her fingers from her mouth, lifted the breast she was fondling, and bowed her head to flick the nipple with her tongue. She repeated the action to her other breast before pinching both nipples hard and moaning.

I was finally able to choke out, "This is fucking awful." As soon as the words were out of my mouth the dizzy spell returned and I sensed something clinging to my backside like a wet silicone blanket. It was clammy and sticky and cold and it forcefully pushed me toward the girl. It was an entity composed of dread and fear and evil and it pressed up against me and held my wrists to direct my arms and slid its feet under my own and took each step for me. The compulsion to bawl was strong but the thing whispered in my ear about my destiny and great pleasures and to give and to receive and the reward would be beyond anything I could imagine if I would do its bidding.

I approached Tryphena. She leaned back on her elbows, unable to lie flat because of the protruding dial board on the back of the machine. I let the presence guide my hands. I slid my hands up her smooth toned thighs. Normally I preferred to give oral to a shaved pussy so I could take my time and tease the exposed skin around the clit. The girl's pubic hair was sparse and once I'd slid my hands up her thighs I parted her with my thumbs. She arched her back and tried to grind against my hands. I slid one hand under and around one thigh and gripped her hip. I inserted two fingers of my other hand inside her. She was extremely wet and cooed as I fingered her in a gentle come-hither gesture to prime her g-spot. She smelled sweet and slightly musky. She squirmed on my fingers and moaned. I let go of her hip and spread her pussy with my thumb and index finger and slowly swirled my tongue around her pink clit before lapping at it. Her come had a bitter taste I recognized as the taste of a girl who smoked. I stole a look up at her as I licked and fingered her. Her head was thrown back and she returned to pinching one of her nipples. I latched onto her clitoris with my mouth and began sucking and flicking it with my tongue. She moaned louder and encouraged me to keep going. I slipped the hand not inside her back under her thigh and up over her stomach and grabbed the breast she wasn't manipulating herself.

"Yes," she said. "Oh yes."

I pinched her nipple and she gasped.

"I'm getting close," she said.

I began finger fucking her harder and faster and buried my face in her cunt and ate her in a frenzy. I realized my erection had returned and I had a strong urge to pull out my cock and masturbate while pleasuring her.

"I'm coming!" she cried out.

Her clit spasmed in my mouth. A gush of her come soaked my hand and splatted onto my neck before pattering on the garage floor. She bucked her hips and slammed her pubis mons into my nose hard enough to make my eyes water. Her clit twitched under the pressure of my tongue as she squirted a second round. Her body convulsed and trembled as the last small waves of her orgasm subsided.

"Fuck me," she said.

I was still manipulating her and I raised my head to look at her. Her expression made me question if she was experiencing ecstasy or anger. The cold clingy presence guiding me did not question her command. I pulled her down from the washer roughly—her skin squealing in protest against the machine's surface—and I forcefully spun her around and bent her over the washer. She made small sounds of protest as I forced her into the position I wanted. I undid my pants quickly and guided my hardened cock into her soaked cunt. She moaned and I grabbed both of her hands and stretched her across the washer's top and made her take hold of the dial board on the back. I grabbed her narrow hips and let the monstrosity controlling me take over. I tried to check out mentally as my body acted against my will but the sounds of her calling out in pleasure and the wet smack-ing noises our bodies made while colliding with as much force as my body could deliver kept me there in the moment as if I were witnessing it all from outside myself. I hammered her pus-sy hard and knew both of us would be bruised. She didn't seem to mind when the impact of my fucking began to ram her into the washer, causing the front of the machine to lift and bang down on the floor. There was no thought in my mind other than a primal animalistic one to procreate and wishing the cold and bothersome puppet master would let go of me but I knew even if the thing would let go I had fallen down a rabbit hole where nothing would ever be the same and I would never be allowed to go home again. The girl moaned in pleasure and looked over her shoulder at me and shouted for me to fuck her harder and I complied and felt a strong orgasm building in my bowels and the panic of whether or not the girl was on birth control crossed my mind for a split second and I knew I needed to pull out but the thing controlling me pressed on my buttocks more forcefully as my orgasm crossed the threshold into the land of no return. I vaguely remember the nauseating expulsion of come as the orgasm gripped my throat, or maybe it was the compelling force choking me. A bolt of sensation exploded and ran from my stomach and into my anus.

17

I was lost in the woods and the sun was setting. With each ticking second I began to panic more and more as I frantically searched for anything that looked remotely familiar, or for a glimpse of another cabin, or the sound of a vehicle to announce a road nearby. In the shadows of the trees the forest was already chilly and I knew it would only get colder once the sun was completely set.

I spotted the flicker of something in the distance through the jumble of trees and used it as a guide as twilight shifted into darkness. I stumbled toward it, branches scraping my arms, legs, and face. It didn't take me long to recognize what I was seeing as a campfire. Once I passed the last cluster of foliage separating me from the campsite I found Tryphena standing by the fire. She was naked. The flames cast ghoulish shadows across her features and the oppressing darkness beyond the light of the fire filled in the blanks and caused her brown eyes to appear as black and luminous as the feathers on a crow.

Something or someone moved in the darkness around us. My mind was filled with the knowledge that whatever was out there was ominous and couldn't touch us until the fire died down and we were swallowed by the night. The thing paced and circled us like a large hungry cat waiting for the prey's moment of weakness so it could pounce and devour what it desired most.

I approached Tryphena and said, "What are you doing here? How do we get home?"

"He likes you," she said. "We are home. We live with him now."

"Who?"

She wrapped her arms around me and began to kiss me. I could smell and taste clove and ashes on her tongue and my cock began to grow hard. She dropped to her knees and unfastened my pants. She looked up at me and her mouth had morphed into a vagina that glistened in the light from the campfire. She stroked me with one hand and fingered the wet cunt where her mouth used to be before taking my cock into her warm vagina-mouth. The temperature of her was scalding and as she worked the fire began to die. I held the back of her head and began to thrust my hips into her when the effigy constructed of trees and branches I had woken up next to emerged from the darkness and stood in front of me. Its misshapen and faceless head appeared more sinister with the creature now animated. The branches it was made of creaked and groaned against one another as it moved. The thing stooped and inserted one of its long and twisted branch fingers into the girl's actual cunt from behind her as I fucked the cunt that replaced her mouth. It removed its finger and lifted it to its face for a second as if inspecting it before it lifted both of its long and menacing hands and placed them on either side of my face. Slowly, it began to insert its thumbs into my eyes.

Darkness enveloped me in a snap as the creature destroyed my vision. Water trickled down the back of my throat and I began to cough and gag. My mouth filled with the coppery taste of blood and I began to drown.

The cough started small and became invasive and hacking before I rolled onto my side and opened my eyes. I was in my bed, fully clothed, and the sunlight was fading fast outside. I covered my mouth and coughed some more. My hand was wet when I pulled it away. I looked at my palm and found it was covered in blood. I sat up in a panic and blood poured from both of my nostrils, down my face, and dripped from my chin. There was blood on the duvet cover from where I had apparently collapsed without turning down the covers. What I had done to Tryphena came rushing back and the memory was followed by a wave of nausea.

I cupped my hand under my chin and proceeded to the bathroom. The mirror above the sink reflected the horror and the panic I was feeling. Partly from the gushing nosebleed I was experiencing and partly from remembering what had happened with Tryphena. I'd only experienced a bloody nose one other time in my life after a scuffle on the playground in elementary school when a bully decided it was his job to rough up any new kids. During the grappling match the kid managed to elbow me in the nose and luckily hadn't managed to break it. Now I leaned over the sink like the school nurse had instructed me back then. Blood dripped into the sink as I turned on the water and adjusted the temperature. I washed the blood from my face and rinsed my mouth before pinching my nose. I continued to lean forward and watched the last of the pinkish water drain away. After what felt like an exorbitant amount of time I let go of my nose and waited to see if it was done bleeding. I retrieved the Q-tips and used a handful soaked in water to clean inside my nostrils. I was afraid to blow my nose in case it provoked another deluge of blood.

Once I was finished cleaning up I turned to the toilet to relieve my bladder. My penis was tacky and I could smell the unmistakable scent of sex coming from it. And then there was no mistake or telling myself maybe I hadn't defiled an underage girl and it was only a fucked up dream when the slight sting of an after sex piss announced itself.

"Fuck," I said aloud. *What the fuck did I do?* I thought. *And what the fuck happened afterward? How did I end up in my own bed? What fucking time was it? Was it even the same day?*

The guilt was crushing. I fought back tears and panic and nausea as I chanted in my head there was no way I was going to allow it to happen again. But promising not to let it happen again was a terrifying thought in itself. Would refusing her again piss her off and cause her to accuse me of pedophilia or rape? She surely had evidence of our coupling on her clothes and in her body now. I think I came in her. I wasn't sure. I barely remembered the orgasm and I was certain I passed out during it. I didn't even know the girl's exact age but I was certain she was *not* eighteen. But I couldn't blame Tryphena for what happened. I was the adult in the situation. If I would have been thinking clearly I would've denied her regardless of her threats. The only semen they would've found on her was possibly her father's. I should've dragged her back to her father's house and waited until Lloyd got home and explained what his daughter was up to. But that was a shitty situation too. I didn't know the status of the report I'd sent to the child protective services. If they had come and gone and things had already been resolved I didn't want to have to interact with Lloyd at all. There weren't many people to point a finger at when you lived with the victim and there was only one other person a stone's throw away who may be one of the few people who saw the girl. Returning her to her father and tattling on her didn't bode well for either Tryphena or me.

I wasn't left with a lot of options. Moving was the best solution. The quicker, the better. The thought of moving broke my heart though. I liked the cabin. I wanted to stay as long as possible. Not to mention I didn't have the money to move again or to pay rent. The only place I could go was back to Phillip's, a place where I didn't feel welcome.

None of this would've happened if Naomi wasn't such a selfish cunt, I thought. The thought actually surprised me. It was the first time since we had separated I was aware of the amount of hatred and contempt I felt for her for deciding I wasn't cut from the right material and was of a lesser quality than some other schlub who would fuck her and marry her and sit around eating Doritos and getting fat with her while he watched the big game every weekend and their brats screamed and fought and cried over toys. And I thought back to the last time Naomi and I had

had sex and how it had been extremely routine and lackadaisical as she lay on her back and we fucked in the missionary position and at some point I opened my eyes and looked at her and she was staring back at me with a bored expression and I knew it was over. I wasn't completely sure it was the very last time we had sex but it was definitely the moment I realized how hollow our relationship was and how she wasn't interested in anything emotional from me anymore. She only wanted to own superficial things: cars, a house, kids. She wanted to own things she could control. She should've just gotten a dog.

Once I was done in the bathroom I checked out the window by the sink and had to crane my head to get a glimpse of the other cabin. There was barely enough daylight left to recognize Lloyd's station wagon was parked in its normal spot. Dim lights flickered in the windows of his cabin. I cracked the window and listened intently for any sounds coming from the other cabin but was only met with the sounds of night insects preparing for a long night of scuttling and singing.

I left the bathroom and realized the background and lighting were still up from Rachel's shoot. I made quick work of tearing it down and stowing it. When I was finished I spotted the dark stain of blood on the duvet. I turned on the lights for the deck and stairs and double checked to make sure Lloyd wasn't waiting outside my door to ambush me and beat me to a pulp or shoot me in the face. I retrieved my laptop and did a quick search on how to wash out bloodstains. I noticed a couple of messages but ignored them momentarily. I briefly thought about how searching bizarre things like how to remove bloodstains probably red flagged some agency and put my name on some list of potentially fucked up people somewhere. I followed the recommendations I found online and soaked the cover and duvet in cold water before scrubbing it with some dish soap and taking it down to the garage to launder.

The garage door was shut and the light had been shut off. I tried not to think about what happened on the washer or look at the dried whitish spot on the floor where Tryphena had squirted. Once the washer was loaded and started I held the laundry detergent lid under the water to fill it and dumped it on the spot on the floor before retreating back inside.

My stomach growled when I stepped inside. My phone sat on the dresser but the battery was dead. I plugged it in to charge. I opened the laptop on the coffee table and checked the time. It was shortly after nine in the evening. There was an email from Phillip asking how things were coming along with the kitchen. I'd completely forgotten I had taken a few photos once I finished it and meant to email them to him. There was a notification for the social networking site. It was a brief message from Rachel saying she had a good time today and was looking forward to hanging out tomorrow. I groaned audibly and rubbed my face wearily. I growled in frustration and tried to think of how to reply to her and began to mentally flog myself for everything that had happened with Tryphena. I really wanted to see Rachel again but now I felt like a despicable human being and she deserved better. I stared at the computer screen for half an hour before typing: "I had fun too and I can't wait to see you again." I deleted the 'I can't wait to see you again' and changed it to 'I can't wait to get some fresh air on the trails and talk' before I sent the message. Less than thirty seconds later a smiley face emoticon appeared in the message box. I stared at the smiley face for a while until the tiny yellow face twisted into a mocking grin.

My stomach protested loudly and demanded food. The stress of everything was beginning to give me a tension headache and my neck was stiff. My nerves were fried and for some reason the skin on my shoulders and back were sore. I rubbed my shoulder and tried to think of a reasonable answer to fix the mess I'd made of my life.

I carried the laptop into the kitchen and sat it on the table. I stared at the computer for a minute, trying to remember why I'd brought it to the table before I remembered to retrieve the camera and the cord to connect to it. My brain was slow to think of much else beyond my dilemma. My thoughts became as muddled as they did when I was severely sleep deprived. I hooked up the camera and made a sandwich as the photos uploaded to my editing program. I tended to get lost in editing and decided it would be a better alternative than worrying until I was sick or had a nervous breakdown. I sat at the table and ate my sandwich while scrolling through the photos of Rachel. I had a hard time deleting the ones not quite up to par. She struck me as saint-like. I wasn't sure why I thought of her that way. But deleting any of her photos felt sacrilegious. I created a new folder on my computer and dropped the rejected photos from the set into it.

I found the few photos I'd taken of the remodeled kitchen and opened my email. I replied to Phillip's email with the kitchen photos attached. I briefly told him about Rachel and the scheduled hike tomorrow and asked him how things were with him before sending the email and returning to the photos.

I ran my finger over the scroll bar a couple of times to advance to the next page of photos. My stomach sank as I stared at what I thought were mistaken and fucked up photos. My first thought was I zoomed in too much on Rachel's hands and the rows of thumbnails were filled with the flesh of her hands with no background. It took a few seconds longer than necessary for my fogged brain to connect the photos to the content. They were blurry and at odd angles and their main foci were on breasts and a vagina. The recognition that they were Tryphena's breasts and vagina hit me a lot quicker and I began to panic. I scrolled through the rest of the photos and their content progressively became more pornographic. At some point she must have figured out how to run the timer. There were full nude shots of her on my bed. Then there were a few pictures of her masturbating on my bed. And a shot of me naked on the bed. One of my face. My eyes were open but only the whites were visible, as if I was having some type of seizure. A picture of the scar on my chest. A photo of an orgasmic Tryphena crouched over my head with her pussy on my mouth. Another photo was staged to look as if we were both orally pleasuring each other. Tryphena riding me reverse cowgirl while pinching her nipples.

In a panic I highlighted the photographs and deleted them and followed it by dumping the trash folder completely. *Fuck! I had child pornography on my computer!* I thought. I began to hyperventilate as I thought about television programs and online articles I'd read that stated even if you delete something from your computer the experts could still recover it. I wanted to smash my computer into a million pieces and set it on fire. But the fucking computer and the camera were my livelihood and I didn't have the money to replace them. I yanked the cord from my camera, turned it on, and was forced to clear each photo one at a time. When I reached the photo of me on the bed alone a thought struck me . . . I was naked. I woke up fully clothed. My brain tried to process the information and I suddenly realized how bad my head was throbbing.

I retreated to the bathroom and took two Tylenol as I tried to piece together in my mind the photos of me and Tryphena. I had no memory of the photos. And obviously by my state in the picture I was having some sort of episode or maybe she drugged me somehow. Then there was the question of my clothes. I had been in a semi-state of dress during our encounter in the garage. That meant either she or I had taken all my clothes off and redressed me. By my condition in the photos it didn't appear there was any way it could've been me. And Tryphena was a slight girl. It didn't seem feasible she would have been able to do it alone.

A wave of nausea hit me and I sprinted to the bathroom and vomited what little of the sandwich I'd managed to consume and the partially dissolved Tylenol. I sat on the bathroom floor by the toilet and cried harder than any time I could ever remember. I didn't think I would ever stop sobbing and eventually forced myself to take a shower to try and soothe my hysterics and hoped I could somehow scrub my soul clean.

18

I showered until there was nothing left but cold water. Afterward I checked the refrigerator and found I only had two beers left and knew those wouldn't be enough to numb my brain into unconsciousness. Even if I did have enough beer my stomach was knotted and hurt. I wasn't sure if I had heartburn or a sour stomach but my intestinal issues were partially from being tortured by my conscience and I didn't have anything in the medicine cabinet to treat my discomfort. I decided I had to go to the store regardless of how terrified I was to leave the sanctity of my home and take a chance Lloyd was lurking in the dark by my car with an axe.

I had to build up the courage twice to walk down to the garage and swap the comforter from the washer to the dryer and retrieve it to put back on the bed. Amazingly, there wasn't a trace of my nosebleed anywhere on it. Once the comforter was done I cautiously double checked out the windows and craned my head in the bathroom window to see Lloyd's cabin. It appeared all of his lights were out and I thought it was probably the best time to leave. My stomach wasn't feeling any better and I had the notion it wouldn't until I took some antacids.

It was close to one in the morning when I finally grabbed my wallet, phone, and keys and convinced myself to creep out of the cabin. My paranoia was wound tight and I almost jumped out of my skin at every small sound as I made my way to the car. Once I was inside the vehicle I quickly locked the doors, started it, and zipped out of the parking spot and down the drive and onto the road toward the twenty-four hour store.

My muscles relaxed once I was a few miles away from home. I hadn't realized how tense I was until then and how hard I was gripping the steering wheel. I preoccupied my mind with watching the tree line for any wandering night creatures as I drove to town. I couldn't afford to fix my car if a deer or some other large animal decided to tango with it. Liability insurance only got you so far. And I needed my car.

There were only a few stray cars in the parking lot of the store. I retrieved a cart and made my way to the pharmacy first. There were myriad stomach medications ranging in symptom relief and combos of discomfort. I decided on a bottle of chewable antacids, a box of pills good for a sour stomach and diarrhea, the latter of which I did not have but figured I'd better be safe than sorry, and a twenty-four hour heartburn reliever. I dropped a small bottle of melatonin into the cart for good measure before crossing the store to the grocery side. I added some beer and a bag of French fries to the cart—because Mom always fed us fries when we had an upset stomach and told us the starch would soothe it—before heading to the checkout.

I grabbed a bottle of water from a cooler at the head of the checkout lane and placed all of my purchases on the belt. The young female clerk eyed me dubiously and asked to check my ID once she scanned the alcohol. The biggest wave of paranoia washed over me as she scrutinized my photo and birthday on my license. I felt as though this young girl, probably not much older than twenty-one, could see the taint of a newly minted sexual deviant radiating from me. Like there was a blinking light on my forehead or a spontaneous new class endorsement on my driver's license indicating to the world I was a thirty-year-old creep who had sex with underage girls. Or maybe Tryphena told Lloyd and he called the police and there was a warrant out for my arrest. I imagined a police officer carrying a photo of me into every local store and telling the employees to keep an eye out for the pervert in the photo and to call them if I happened to show up in their store. But that was ludicrous. If Lloyd informed the police and they had a warrant out for me they also knew where I lived and I would've already been sitting in a jail cell. Unless the police were waiting to catch me in the act of trying to lure some other unsuspecting teen girl into having sex with me. Or more likely, in the age of reality television, they were jockeying to get their cameras into position and waiting for Chris Hansen to arrive. The stress of what if, what if, what if, was beginning to make my head throb again.

The checkout girl finally handed back my ID and her brief glance at my face made me feel shameful and embarrassed as if I were caught doing something I knew better than to do and her silent assessment of me was a reprimand. She finished ringing up my items without a word. I paid and quickly exited the store.

Once I was to my car I opened the medicines for the stomach issues and took the recommended dosage for each one. I chewed the chalky tablets last. The bottle claimed they were fruit flavored but they actually tasted like unflavored Kool-Aid powder. I drank all the water, swishing each large swallow to remove the gritty antacids stuck in the crevices of my molars.

The medicine went to work almost immediately. The pain in my stomach dulled some but there was a residual ache telling me the situation wasn't completely over and the pain could come raging back any moment.

A police car pulled into the parking lot and I decided it was time to leave. I cautiously drove to the exit, using the assigned aisles and not crossing the parking spaces, constantly checking my rearview mirrors to see if the cop was following me. The police car parked in a spot near the door and shut its lights off. At the last second I decided to turn in the opposite direction of home and head into town. I didn't know what driving into town would accomplish if the cop had chosen to follow me other than to make me look more like a creep for stalking around a town I didn't live in in the middle of the night.

I took the turns necessary to pass the post office. Farther down the same road I passed a plain block church with a wooden sign out front with lopsided hand-painted service hours. Normally I would turn onto the road in front of the church to head back home after I was done at the post office but I decided to continue on. I had never explored much of the town beyond the basic relevant to me: store, post office, library, hardware store, eating establishments. I drove past rows of tiny houses with adequate yards. The majority of them had darkened windows and the streets were abandoned and dotted with street lights positioned too far apart to do much good. A few of the houses' windows flickered and flashed in accordance to the televisions playing within them. I barely made out the silhouette of a looming and bowlegged figure standing statuesque in the front yard of one darkened home with an overgrown yard. A small dog jumped and barked furiously at me a few feet in front of the figure and as my car approached the boorish figure yanked on what I assumed was a leash. The dog yelped in pain and the figure scolded the creature before lumbering back toward their house, dragging the dog with them.

After a few blocks of houses I spotted a cemetery on the right side of the road and a large ornate church built on a small incline was located across from it. The beautiful stained glass windows were lit and a lone car sat in the parking lot. I pulled into the lot to turn around and head home but spotted the church's marquee sign. It read St. John's Catholic Church with the message 'open any time' spelled out with flimsy plastic letters along with the time their masses were held. I decided to park my car and get out.

I wasn't raised Catholic. In fact, Mom never took Phillip and me to any church. I couldn't remember a time God was mentioned in our house growing up other than to swear. I didn't blame her for choosing not to force an outdated set of rules and morals on my brother and I. Whether it was because of her lack of faith, or loss of it, I didn't know. And I didn't fault my absence of religion for anything that had happened or could happen to me. Everything that was happening to me, or had occurred throughout my life, was established by my own choice or by chance. Because if I was forced to believe there was a higher and all powerful entity pulling the strings then I firmly believed that higher being was a fucking evil and malicious asshole.

I approached the main entrance of the church. A light shone brightly above the two massive wooden doors. There was a painting of Christ above the door with an eagle perched on his shoulder as if the artist's interpretation of the holy man was confused with a pirate. I checked one of the doors and, like the sign out front stated, it was open. I slipped inside quietly and found a few candles flickering inside the entrance along with a font holding holy water. The ceiling was massive and ran close to three or four stories tall. I didn't spot anyone else and I approached the holy water. I dipped my fingers in it and was shocked to realize it didn't feel any different than tap water left out on the counter until it reached room temperature. I wasn't sure what I'd expected. For it to be hot? Cold? To act as an acid and melt my heretic fingers down to the bone? I cupped my hand and gathered a small amount of the water in my palm before stooping over the bowl to drink it. I waited to be struck by lightning or to spontaneously combust or for anything to tell me there was someone out there who gave a shit and there was a way to right everything that had gone so very wrong.

Nothing.

I left the church disappointed and drove toward home. I made it out of town and was halfway home when I noticed a presence in the car. I checked my rearview mirror and saw my father's face, illuminated by the dash lights, sitting in the back seat. I started from the shock and almost drove off the road. A part of me wanted to scream and freak out but something silent in my brain informed me I knew this was a part of the overall picture. I pulled the car to the shoulder of the road and stopped. I stared at my father's reflection, the man who had taken his own life at the very same age I was now, as he assessed me in the mirror. My breath was coming and going in giant swallows and exhalations.

"Are you really shocked to see me?" he said.

"I don't know," I huffed.

He shook his head. "It's going to end soon."

I squeezed my eyes shut and opened them again, wondering if there *was* something in the holy water or if I was experiencing hallucinations brought on by stress or lack of sleep or both. I turned in my seat to find my father still sitting in the back seat. I fumbled on the dash until I found the switch for the dome light and flipped it on. I turned back to my father and he was every bit as solid as any other human being on earth. I also noticed he had a grayish pallor and there was a purple and yellow bruise encircling his neck. I could make out the features of his face here and there he'd passed onto Phillip but there was an unsettling in my stomach as I realized in another time or place my father and I could've passed as twins. There were a few things differentiating us from one another. His brow was a little thicker. His chin was slightly wider. This similarity wasn't a complete shock though. I vaguely remembered my father from my childhood and my mother kept a few small photos of him on display while we were growing up but it had been a while since I'd seen any of the photos and I hadn't compared myself to him then. Now I was seeing him and I as equals in age. And seeing someone who resembled me so closely in such a ghastly light made the skin on the back of my neck pull straight on end hard enough to make my back teeth hurt and feel loose.

"How?" I managed to spit out.

He smiled wearily and shrugged.

"Why?" I said.

"I don't know. This is about you."

"Are you a ghost?"

Again, he shrugged.

I turned around in my seat to face forward. I said, "Why did you do it?" I looked up into the rearview mirror and the back seat was empty. I turned quickly to search the back seat and he was gone. I did a couple of confused double takes and found myself in the car alone.

I rubbed my sweaty face, trying to piece together what had happened. I spotted the plastic sack of heartburn and sour stomach medicine I'd purchased. I snagged up the bag, dug through it in a frenzy, and quickly read each of the drug's side effects. There were no indicators the medication had provoked what had taken place or if mixing them or taking too many would cause hallucinations. I threw the bag back on the passenger seat, turned the dome light off, and continued home to drink a few beers and try to sleep before Rachel arrived. And I was beginning to wonder if an extensive doctor bill wasn't a bad idea.

19

I didn't sleep well even with the assistance of a couple of beers. When I did sleep it wasn't for long and I had terrible nightmares. I continually rehashed my worries while lying awake in the dark. I couldn't stop thinking about how either Lloyd was going to kill me or I was going to end up in a padded room. I kept thinking about the vision of my father and whether he was a stress-induced figment of my imagination or a ghost and knew a psychological examination was a good idea. But I didn't have any money or health insurance and I didn't believe in the supernatural. I tried to force my brain to classify my experience as an otherworldly phenomenon because it was the cheapest treatment. You could choose to ignore it or contact an exorcist to take care of it. Convincing myself it was supernatural left me to question everything I believed in and cemented my fear that I was on the brink of madness. And if I wasn't fretting over what I'd seen I was terrified for my life or of going to jail because of what had happened with Tryphena. I knew ignoring her wouldn't solve anything. The thing that bothered me the most was all my worries eating all my thoughts and keeping me from feeling the normal nervousness and sleeplessness of potentially spending an afternoon with Rachel. I would've gladly taken the stress and worries that accompany hanging out with a girl I really liked.

I forwent trying to get any more sleep once the sun rose and the clock on my cellphone read nine in the morning. I decided the best thing to do was to get up and keep my mind occupied with a daily routine. I ate, showered, shaved, dressed, and paced the cabin. Thoughts of Rachel kept me antsy. I racked my brain for a way to deal with Tryphena and decided the best thing I could do was to never tell another soul about it. I wasn't one for secrets. It's not that I couldn't keep a secret. I could. It was just I'd never held anything back from anyone I was in a relationship with. I wasn't sure what was happening between me and Rachel but if we did become a thing, and God knows I wanted it to, I didn't know how I felt about holding something like this back.

There was a knock on the door a few minutes before noon and my nervousness peaked. My palms were sweating like mad and I wiped them on my jeans before opening the door. Rachel stood on the deck, all smiles. Her hair was pulled into a messy ponytail. She wore a thin white T-shirt and I could see the shadow of her black bra through the material. She also wore a pair of cutoff denim shorts and a pair of tennis shoes. I held the screen door for her to enter.

"Are you ready?" she said.

"I think so."

She thumbed over shoulder. "I got us a couple of bottles of water."

"That's probably a good idea."

The cat was asleep on his pillow. I scooped him up and took him to the back door. He looked up at me sleepily and indignantly when I set him on the deck. I shut the door and locked it before grabbing my keys and wallet.

"Ready," I said.

She nodded and led the way. I couldn't take my eyes from the lithe muscles of her legs as they flexed with each step and tried desperately to think of anything other than sex. My nervous energy quickly transformed into a thick sexual tension . . . at least on my part. I had no idea what Rachel's intentions were. I only knew what I wanted them to be and how I was interpreting our exchange and time together with the absence of the guise of partners working as a photographer and model.

My heart was hammering by the time we reached the top of the stairs. I dreaded the thought of seeing Tryphena standing on the porch smoking and her observing me leaving with Rachel and how Tryphena would process Rachel and I together and whether or not she would choose the moment to cause a mortifying scene. But there was no one outside Lloyd's and my panic subsided some.

Rachel headed toward her car.

"I can drive if you want," I said.

"That's okay. I've passed the place a couple of times and know where it is."

"Are you sure?"

"Yeah," she said and opened the driver's door of her car. "It looked busy when I passed it on the way here. The parking lot was full and people were parking along the side of the road."

I proceeded around the back of her car and adjusted my erection. I was going to have to deal with this again. Being around Rachel made me feel like an oversexed teenager. I situated myself in the passenger seat to keep my pants from pinching my hard on and plucked the bottom of my T-shirt to cover my embarrassing erection.

We didn't talk much on the way to our destination and the place wasn't far from my cabin. She was right. The warm summer day lured a lot of people to the trailhead and there were signs pointing people toward the waterfall and another set of signs directing people to a large cave. We were forced to park on the side of the road. Rachel handed me a bottle of water from a bag in the back seat before exiting the car. She said she wanted to see the waterfall first.

We walked around the overflowing parking lot and took a short trail toward a set of wide stairs constructed out of fallen timber and packed earth. We passed people in groups climbing the stairs and I was amazed at how many of the women wore flimsy sandals that didn't appear to be a good option for climbing stairs constructed out of compressed mud. The stairs descended a couple hundred feet and stopped alongside a shallow and slow moving stream. We stopped to catch our breath and moved out of the way so other people could pass. I took a couple of gulps of water before we proceeded to a bridge that passed over the stream and led us toward the waterfall. While crossing the bridge I spotted several people wading in the water and stacking rocks. There were piles of rocks everywhere in the stream and it appeared to be a type of tradition or game that had been ongoing for a long time. We could see the waterfall from a short distance and came to a packed clearing by the pool of the fall. People were everywhere. Children were running around and playing in the water. There was a plaque mounted on a giant stone carved to look like a podium. Rachel approached it and I followed her. It was a brief history of the park and the waterfall and a request for visitors to refrain from entering the water to keep from disturbing the fragile ecosystem. I refrained from making a snide comment about how the rules apparently didn't apply to about fifty percent of the people here. I didn't want Rachel to see my snarky side yet.

Rachel gave a hard look to a woman standing in the water in a swimsuit. The woman was a few feet from a large wooden sign with the words 'no swimming' carved into it in large capital letters. Apparently she was thinking the same thing I was. A group of people stood up from a large rock by the water's edge and took their leave.

Rachel grabbed my hand and pulled gently. "Come on," she said.

Her touch sent a warm rush through my body. I followed her and expected her to drop my hand but she held onto it until we reached the rock. We took a seat facing the waterfall. The crash of the water into the pool created a damp cool breeze at this proximity. And I couldn't stop thinking about whether or not I should take up her hand again. I was never good at reading women and always left it to them to make the first move.

"Isn't this nice?" she said. She turned her face up toward the top of the waterfall.

The cacophony of people talking and children playing mixed with the rush of the waterfall made it difficult to hear her. I moved closer to her to talk without shouting but still left a small distance between us as to not make her feel uncomfortable.

"It is," I said. "I should've come here before." I thought, *This would be a nice place to hang out in the off season or during the week when it wasn't overrun with inconsiderate people.* I stared at the couple of inches of empty space between her hip and mine before looking up at the waterfall with her. "I've been so busy. I haven't taken any time to explore the park."

She turned to me. "Does the photography take up a lot of time?"

I chuckled and looked at her. I wanted to stare at her all day. I decided to rest my gaze on an empty part of the pool. "No," I said. "I've been working on the cabin. It was my mother's. I just came out of a breakup and my brother and I decided I could live there rent free in exchange for remodeling it. We're going to sell it once I've found a new place to live."

Hesitantly, she said, "*Was* your mother's cabin?"

"Yeah. She passed away."

A pained expression passed over her face and she opened her mouth to say something but I stopped her.

"It's okay," I said. "It's been a while."

She shyly asked, "Your dad?"

"He uh . . ." I took a deep breath. Telling people your father committed suicide was never easy and I'd never quite mastered it. "He killed himself when I was seven."

"Oh, Jesus," she said. "I'm so sorry. I had no idea—"

"It's okay." I gave a nervous laugh. "I'm pretty certain my life was meant to be a Greek tragedy. I try not to let it get me down too much. If you can't laugh at yourself and everything that doesn't go as planned you might as well lock yourself in a closet and scream to the end of eternity. Life will keep happening and there isn't much you can do to change the luck of the draw. My dad's death is like living with a tiny open wound. At first it hurts really bad but eventually you get used to it and it doesn't bother you unless you think about it."

She gave me a sympathetic crooked smile. "What happened with your last relationship? Or should I ask?" She laughed.

"She was using me like a bookmark." I mimicked inserting a bookmark in a wedge with my hands. "Let me put this here for now until I'm ready to live life how I want." I placed my hands on the rock behind me and reclined some. "I filled an empty space for her. I was agreeable and inoffensive. But she didn't want Mr. Right. She wanted Mr. Perfect. I guess she was waiting for someone with the same life goals to come along or something. That's the guy she really wanted to build her life with. Not me. I think she wanted to be a housewife or something."

She nodded her head. "I know a couple of those."

"You?" I said.

She held up her hands. "Being a freak tends to attract freaks." She folded her hands in her lap and stared at them for a moment. "I've kinda put relationships on the backburner. Stag's not so bad. I meet a lot of interesting people. But for the most part they turn into overeager Chihuahuas once they notice the hands and can't discuss much of anything else."

"People are weird."

"Tell me about it. Whenever someone does that I always want to ask them if they'd interrogate someone in a wheelchair about what it's like living in a wheelchair or ask a blind person how they wipe their ass. It seems rude and ignorant to think the only thing the person wants to talk about is their handicap. I'm not saying I'm handicapped or know a tenth of the plight they struggle with but . . ." She held up her hands. "It's like the last thing I want to talk about sometimes. I'd like to have a normal conversation about movies or politics or . . . something without being constantly reminded I have this thing that makes me different, therefore, it must be the determining thing that defines me as a person and constructs my personality."

"That's why I never approach people for photos. I let them come to me."

"You do really well. You have a level of respect and appreciation that's apparent in your photos. They don't come off as exploitative."

We stared at the waterfall for a few seconds.

I said, "Your folks?"

She smiled weakly. "They're okay. They moved to Texas after my sister and I were out of the house. They usually fly up for Christmas every year and stay with my sister and her husband for a week." She wiggled the fingers of her right hand at me. "They're all normal."

A couple of elementary age boys stood in the water up to their knees twenty feet from us. They smacked the water's surface and splashed one another. Rachel watched them. I watched her for a reaction to them. Her expression was indifferent. She didn't appear to hate them or adore them. She watched them the way I imagined she would observe leaves rustling across the ground on a windy day. They were there. They were doing their thing. What they were doing didn't involve her. They would still continue their course of action whether or not she was involved. And there was no connection between the two.

I broke her reverie and said, "No kids?"

"Hm?"

"Do you have kids?"

She laughed. "No."

I observed the boys who stopped splashing each other. The taller of the two chased the other. They marched in the slowed manner of running in water and squealed at each other in delight.

"You have kids?" she asked.

"No." I wasn't going to lie to her. "I don't want kids. It was one among many reasons I wasn't Mr. Perfect."

When I mentioned I didn't want any children I noticed a miniscule softening of her posture.

"Me either," she said. "There's no desire there. I don't think I was born with the nurturing bug. Everyone tells me it kicks in once you have a kid but I don't think it's for me. And I'm fine with that. It seems warped for someone to have a child and expect nature to do its job. What if it didn't? Animals abandon their newborns and leave them for dead all the time."

I nodded and we both fell silent again and observed the people around us. Families and couples milled about and took photos with their phones. A woman in a sun dress directed her three small girls to take a photo of them with the waterfall in the background. A teenaged girl took a selfie with a teen boy I assumed was her boyfriend. I peeked back the way we had come and two men stood in the middle of the bridge holding hands. One of the men held his phone at arm's length to take a photo of the both of them. There were a lot of photos being taken with phones followed by feverish typing on the phone's screens.

"You should have brought your camera." Rachel said.

She must have been observing the same thing I was.

"Yeah," I said. "I never think to bring it to things like this. I always feel like if you're taking a photo you're not really experiencing the thing you're photographing. At least for me. I'm too focused on getting the perfect photo that the image on the screen becomes an abstract and dislocated thing. My mind tunes into the lighting and the angle and the focal point and I lose the pleasure of just being there and committing the experience to memory."

"How did you get into photography?"

"I took a free afterschool program that taught the basics of taking photos and developing thirty-five millimeter film." I smiled at the memory. "We were so poor we didn't even own a camera. The instructor lent me an extra Minolta he had laying around. He must've felt sorry for me. He told me to keep it once I completed the class."

"Is it the camera you used?"

"No. I hocked it when I was younger to pay some bills. Once I got over the financial hump I bought the digital one I have now."

"That sucks."

"Yeah. I wish I still had it. As a keepsake at least. It was all manual. The way everything always goes it's probably considered vintage at this point." I paused briefly. "So what do you do?"

Her expression became pensive and worried. I knew from her online profile she was a painter and a singer but I didn't want to mention I'd already pawed through her online information like a stalker. She appeared to be embarrassed to answer and I assumed she was a self-flagellating artist. Which was a good thing. I always believed an artist should constantly be unhappy with their output. If you were unhappy with your work it pushed you to try harder. An artist who thinks their work is a masterpiece is a delusional artist and not one I wanted to talk to about their craft or mine.

"Well . . ." she drew out. "I like to paint these terrible pictures to line my closets with. And sometimes I do some backup vocals for a friend's band. But I don't make a living from either of those things. Like you. You make a living from art and I adore that."

I chuckled. "Borderline poverty isn't quite a living and shouldn't be revered."

She smiled. "It's better than nothing, right?"

I shrugged. "I guess so."

She paused and bit her lip before leaning closer to me and shyly adding, "I do online . . . porn." Her eyebrows scrunched and she made a pained face as if she were expecting some type of verbal onslaught. She leaned back to her normal spot and looked around to make sure no one nearby heard her. She hurriedly whispered, "I don't have sex with other people." She held up her hands to insinuate them and gave me a chagrined smile. "They attract fetishists who want to watch me pleasure myself." She dropped her hands into her lap and folded them together and began to wring them nervously. "They pay by the minute to interact with me and I don't have any physical contact with them. I work from the privacy of my own home and I'm not forced to do anything I don't want. If something is too creepy or weird I can just close the browser."

I didn't know how to respond. It was the first time I'd met anyone who did porn. I didn't want to come off as a pervert by asking her more about it. And I didn't want her to think I was some type of prude who disapproved by sitting next to her grasping for the right words when nothing could be further from the truth. I was a porn viewer myself. There was something taboo and titillating about her confession that only made me want to fuck her even more. It wasn't the weird fantasy men had about women in porn being more experienced or theatrical or better in bed or willing to go a little further than most women. It was her ability to dominate the situation and control the aspects by being her own boss and it was on her own terms and she realized she could trick men into paying for sex with her without actually having sex with her. Like a snake oil salesman.

My erection suddenly became painful and my balls began to ache with desire. She watched me nervously for a reaction. I had a strong urge to kiss her but thought it wasn't the most appropriate time.

"As long as you're safe," I said awkwardly. "And no one is forcing you. What does it matter?"

We stared at each other for a brief moment and I felt the

heat of embarrassment rise in my cheeks. We both started laughing and I had to look away.

"Most guys either get really excited and want to talk about porn for the next two hours or they turn into assholes because they think I'm a slut. I don't think anyone has responded as nonchalantly as you."

"Well, yeah. I mean . . . if people wanted to give me money to watch me masturbate I'd probably be a millionaire by now. I'd feel like I was pulling the wool over their eyes or something. I'm going to jerk off whether they're watching or not. Might as well make some money from it." I could feel my face flush even more. "I can't believe I just said that." I'd never been so open about my sexual habits with a girl before.

We both laughed. When our laughter died away she unexpectedly leaned in and kissed me. The abruptness didn't give me time to close my eyes and I stared at her long eyelashes as her warm and sweet tongue darted into my mouth. I found myself desperately trying to match the dance and rhythm of her tongue. My heart quickened and I raised my hand to touch her hair as she withdrew from the kiss as quickly as she initiated it.

She looked embarrassed and wouldn't look at me. "Sorry," she said.

My hand still hung in the air about to grasp her hair. "Let's try that again," I said.

She looked at me and I ran my hand into her hair and pulled her into a kiss. I was prepared this time and our tongues found the brand new rhythm of a new lover. The temperature of the breeze dropped drastically, the red darkness of my closed eyes against the sunlight grew gray, and I knew without opening my eyes a cloud had passed over the sun. Goosebumps rose on my arms. She placed a hand high on my thigh close to my hard cock and I let out an involuntary moan. We mutually retreated from the kiss and she removed her hand from my lap.

I pulled my hand from her hair and said, "Now I get to be sorry."

The area steadily grew darker and the wind picked up. A few people had begun to take their leave. The small patch of sky above the tree tops was filled with gray clouds. The other people at the waterfall sensed the coming rain and the families with small children and elderly people were quickly retreating across the bridge and up the stairs.

I said, "It looks like it's going to rain."

Rachel looked up at the sky with me. The dark clouds moved rapidly and one in particular flickered with lightning. A few seconds later a clap of thunder was barely audible over the din of the waterfall.

She said, "I didn't think it was supposed to rain today."

"It's the valley," I said. "The weather is unpredictable. They can call for a high of eighty-five and sunny in the morning and by the end of the day the warmest it got was sixty and it rained all day."

"We should head back to the car."

I agreed and we followed the steady stream of people up the stairs. Halfway to the top the sound of the rustling leaves was replaced with the *pat pat pat* of the first fat raindrops hitting them. A few darkened drops appeared on the dirt stairs and Rachel groaned we were going to get soaked before making it to the car. The line was slow moving as the smallest children and the assisted elderly struggled to climb them. By the time we reached the parking lot it was a downright deluge. Rachel squealed with delight as we ran through the grass surrounding the parking lot. We spotted a woman near the road holding an umbrella over herself and a boy who appeared to be no older than six or seven. The boy vomited whatever brightly colored and sugar laden candy and drink he'd recently consumed. Rachel dug in her pocket for her keys as she approached the car. Her hair and clothing, along with mine, were completely soaked. Her black bra was a dark contrast and now completely visible through her wet white shirt.

We entered her car and used some fast food napkins she had stored in her glove compartment to dry our faces and hands. She started the car and carefully maneuvered through the fleeing traffic and rain toward my house. The rain was falling so hard her windshield wipers worked double time and still were almost unable to keep up. She drove cautiously and at half the speed limit.

I pointed out the driveway as we approached it and I said, "If you drive down there I don't know if you'll be able to get out today. The rain makes the driveway hard to drive up. You can pull over and drop me off. I'm already soaked."

"That's okay," she said with a devilish grin. "I don't mind staying for a while. If you don't mind."

My heartrate went into overdrive. This was happening. This beautiful girl might actually want to have sex with me. Or at the very least make me feel like an uncontrollable beast who can't keep from thinking with his pecker for a couple of hours. *No*, I told myself. *She doesn't want to have sex with you after meet-*

ing you twice. She probably doesn't want to drive around an area she isn't familiar with in terrible weather and sit in a lonely hotel room. She just wants to hang out and talk more instead of watching awful hotel cable shows. You might as well set yourself up for a night of blue balls. I told her to be careful descending the path, held the handle of the car door, and prepared to luge into the ravine.

The trees sheltered us from the brunt of the rain. My stomach sank when we rounded the corner in the drive and a figure could be seen standing on the porch of Lloyd's cabin. Rachel either didn't seem to notice or didn't care as she pulled into the parking spot by my car. She killed the engine and tried to peer up at the sky through her windshield.

She said, "I don't think it's going to let up. We're gonna have to make a run for it."

I tried not to let the guilt and the presence of Tryphena bother me. I couldn't let it bother me. It was done. It was over. It was a mistake. It was never happening again. I had a chance to start anew with Rachel and I was damned if I was going to let some bratty psychopath ruin it or the mood of the day.

"Be careful on the stairs," I said. "They get slick when they're wet." I grabbed the door handle. "On three. One. Two."

Rachel opened her door and squealed as the pouring rain hit her. I followed her lead. I kept my eyes on her and purposely avoided the burning stare of Tryphena. It was as if her gaze was a physical blow I could feel on my skin. Rachel held the rail and carefully descended the stairs. Thunder rumbled lazily in the distance. Rachel's wet shirt clung to her skin and I focused on the curve in the small of her back. Once at the door and sheltered by the roof she gathered her hair and tried to wring the water from it. I unlocked the door and let her enter first.

We kicked off our shoes and peeled off our wet socks and dropped them on the door mat. Little drops of water fell from Rachel's hair as she bent to remove her socks. I retreated to the bathroom and grabbed two towels. When I exited the bathroom I found Rachel in the process of removing her shirt. I stopped dead in my tracks and stared at her like some moron maid service holding the towels. She smiled at me as she tossed her shirt on top of her shoes. Thunder rumbled again as she unfastened her shorts and wiggled out of them to reveal gray and black striped bikini underwear. She tossed the shorts on the pile of wet clothes she was creating and crossed the cabin to me. I held out a towel for her, not knowing what to do. She took it and dropped it on the floor. She grabbed the other towel I was holding and threw it on the floor also. She placed her hands on either side of my face and kissed me. She pressed her body into mine and there was no need for my body to react. I was hard. I held the small of her back and kissed her until she began to tug at my shirt.

I pulled off my shirt and tossed it into the bathroom. Her eyes fell on the scar on my chest and I had a panic attack. The fear of the scar souring the mood caused my balls to tighten. I debated trying to explain it right then and there before she calculated I was a psychopath and decided to leave. I opened my mouth but before I could say anything her mouth was on mine again and she was fumbling with the button and zipper of my pants.

Rain pelted the roof and my panic peaked when she finally lowered my zipper. There was always a part of me that wanted to scream in terror the first time I ever had sex with a girl. I wanted to fuck the girl so bad and couldn't think of anything else but slipping my cock inside her. But in those three seconds before she actually saw my cock my brain always screamed 'oh god what if she thinks it's too small or weird looking or I'm a terrible fuck' and then it's over and my dick is out and she doesn't care and she still wants to fuck me. At least that's how it has always ended previously. And like that, Rachel sprung me free of my wet pants and underwear and was stroking me and kissing me and I began to struggle to completely remove my wet pants and underwear as they protested and clung to my legs. I broke our kiss and embarrassingly hopped around until I was liberated from my clothing while Rachel watched and giggled at me as she unfastened and removed her bra to reveal small firm breasts with hard nipples.

She walked backward toward the bed and sat. I bent to kiss her. She maneuvered back on the bed and I followed her, our mouths locked together the whole time. She grabbed my cock and stroked it, nearly pulling me over the edge. I pulled my mouth from hers and licked and kissed along her neck. She let go of my cock. Her skin tasted earthy from the rainwater and it seemed appropriate as the thunderstorm outside was the soundtrack for what was happening. I teased her already hardened nipples with my tongue as she moaned, biting one lightly until she gasped. I trailed my tongue down to her bellybutton as her stomach muscles tightened and she laughed softly. I looked up to her and she smiled down at me. She ran her fingers into my wet hair and I took it as an approval to eat her pussy.

I rose to my knees and she eyed my cock as I grabbed either

side of her wet panties and removed them. Her pussy was hairless and I felt like I'd hit a jackpot. I loved to orally pleasure a woman and nothing was more enticing than one who was freshly shaved. I slid down on the bed and repositioned my dick before lying on my stomach. Her cunt smelled intoxicating and I tentatively began to eat her while watching her for a negative or positive reaction to my technique. She cooed and stroked my hair and I slid a finger into her wet pussy and manipulated her. My erection was becoming more painful with each passing minute and Rachel's moans increased.

After a few minutes she said, "I want to fuck you."

I withdrew my fingers from her and sucked her juices from them as she sat up. She got on all fours and directed me to lie on my back. I repositioned to lie on my back on the bed with a pillow under my head. She mounted me and guided my cock into her slowly. I groaned as she rode me slowly. She placed her hands on my chest to steady herself and I was only vaguely aware one of her hands was on the scarred symbol. I grabbed her waist as she worked and resisted the urge to lift my hips and thrust into her and fuck her as hard as I possibly could until I came.

She suddenly dismounted me, spun around reverse cowgirl, and reinserted my cock into her pussy. She bent forward, putting pressure on my cock, and gently caressed my balls before sliding her hand to her clit to stimulate herself. I grabbed her ass cheeks to spread them and peered down to watch my slick dick slide in and out of her cunt while she rode me. Her thrusts began to slow and she masturbated herself faster. I licked one of my thumbs and pressed it against her anus. She cooed louder and I took it as an approval. I slowly began to press the tip of my thumb into her anus and she suddenly cried out. Her pussy spasmed around my cock as she orgasmed. She bucked her hips and rode my cock while stroking herself. She placed a hand on the bed behind her and leaned back. She flipped her head back to look at me upside down before slapping her own clit loudly and moaning. She lay back on me and I ran my hand over the hand she was masturbating with. She removed her hand and allowed me to rub her clit for her. I squeezed one of her taut nipples with my free hand as she wriggled and moaned and tried to fuck me.

I couldn't take the buildup anymore. I sat up and, in doing so, forced her to sit too. She made a surprised and confused sound and I asked her to lie flat on her stomach. She complied in a teasing way by starting on her hands and knees and slowly lowering herself and made sure to make her ass the prominent feature. I stroked myself slowly as I watched her. She crossed her hands in front of her face and laid her head on them, her face turned to the side to watch me over her shoulder. I straddled her thighs and she lifted her ass slightly and smiled at me. I guided my cock into her cunt, grabbed her hips, and began to fuck her with everything I had. She slipped one of her hands under her and began to masturbate herself again. She made pained faces at me over her shoulder as I fucked her. I felt my orgasm building deep in my bowels and suddenly the question of birth control crossed my mind.

I slowed down and whispered, "Is it okay if I come in you?"

"Oh, yes, please, I'm coming again! Please fuck me!"

I didn't need any more direction. She moaned loudly and repeated 'oh fuck' a few times as I jackhammered her with everything I had. My orgasm was so sudden and strong the release was painful and made me nauseated. I collapsed on top of her to catch my breath but didn't put all of my weight on her. I panted on the back of her neck as she cooed. My penis began to shrink inside of her and I withdrew from her and lay on my back beside her.

Still on her stomach she propped herself up on her elbows and looked at me. She smiled and I think I might have fallen in love with her, exposed and vulnerable in post coitus. It felt unreal to be with such a beautiful girl. A faint beam of sunlight tried to shine through the window by the bed and I realized the storm had passed and the sound of rain pattering on the roof was water dripping from the trees.

I touched her hair and said, "I don't feel like I deserve this."

Her eyes darted away from mine in an embarrassed expression and her smile faded as I recognized she was looking at the scar on my chest. I stared at her face as she reached for my scar and ran her fingers over the smooth lines of the symbol. She appeared concerned and confused.

"What happened?" she said.

I didn't want to lie to her. "Uh." I struggled to come up with a way to explain it. "I was having some issues and . . . I'm not sure why I did it—"

"Are you a cutter?" She looked me over for any additional scars.

"No. I don't know what happened. I can get pretty self-loathing sometimes but I've never been one to hurt myself. Obviously there's a family history of mental illness but . . ." I shrugged. "It was dumb. I'm not suicidal. It's kinda embarrassing."

She traced the lines and said, "It looks like a symbol. Does it mean anything?"

"Not that I'm aware of." I searched her concerned face as she stared at the scar. "Please don't think I'm crazy. I'm pretty certain it was caused by an episode of high stress and lack of sleep and—"

"It's okay," she said. "I don't think you're crazy."

"You said you had to deal with weirdos and I don't want you to think I'm one of them."

"Not even close," she said.

She kissed me and I started to become aroused again. It had been years since I was able to bounce back so quickly. She rolled onto her back and began to stoke her cunt.

"Again," she whispered.

She didn't have to tell me twice.

20

After we were done having sex the second time we retreated to the bathroom to shower together, which quickly led into her fellating me after we were finished. She playfully and slowly manipulated my cock while she masturbated. I didn't think there would be anything left in me after the third time but she was able to coax me into fucking her while she bent over the back of the sofa.

She dug through my dresser and found a pair of pajama pants with a drawstring waist I hardly ever wore and a worn tank top of mine to wear while I laundered her clothes. I made spaghetti and garlic toast for supper. When her clothes were dry I brought them upstairs but she continued to wear my clothing.

We sat on the deck and talked about each other's childhood. I told her about what it was like being raised with an older brother and by a single mom and how the three of us worked hard and together to keep the household afloat. She told me about her parents who had both worked factory jobs and how she and her sister were latchkey kids like Phillip and I. We had more in common than we both expected. When you were left to your own devices at an early age you discover how self-sufficient you can be and there isn't any need for anyone else. It caused your relationships to suffer for the rest of your life until you met someone who'd been raised the same way.

There were other things we shared. Like being an outsider among your peers. She had difficulty being accepted amongst schoolmates because of her hands and it was the reason she forwent going to college. I had difficulty making friends because I was poor and was lucky to be at any one given school for the full year. Granted, her situation was far more hurtful in the development of a person's social growth but we both had a good dose of what it was like to be alone aside from one sibling.

We talked about the horrors and tortures of having an older sibling and laughed at how important we thought our childhood worries were back then. We began to drink beer after night fell and toasted to failed relationships. The cat eventually joined us on the deck as we drank and talked and he took to lying in Rachel's lap and allowed her to pet him. Once it grew late and we both had a good beer buzz and were sleepy we retreated into the cabin. The cat joined us.

We settled into bed and I spooned her but our cuddling graduated into groping as we both sought each other in the dark. We had sex lazily in the darkness and my orgasm cleared the beer haze from my brain momentarily. Before falling asleep I thought about how tacky our naked skin felt against one another and how I would probably wake up sweating from her body heat and how lucky I was to meet her and for once I'd met someone who made me feel comfortable in my own skin and it was serene.

21

I felt moving pinpoints of pressure on my chest. Something fuzzy tickled my nose and dragged me from a dreamless sleep. The fuzz solidified into something hard under my nose and forced itself past my lips and into my mouth. The points of pressure on my chest rooted themselves to gain leverage and force the fuzziness deeper into my mouth.

Panic cleared the sleep and leftover beer from my brain. My mouth was stretched wide and the hard furry thing blocked my throat and my ability to breathe. In the darkness I grasped at the object entering my mouth. Once I had my hands around it I knew I had ahold of the cat. He buried his claws into my neck and chest and forced himself deeper into my throat. The scratches burned like acid and I thrashed and tore at him to get him to stop. The pain as the cat forced himself into my throat was unbearable and I flopped around on the bed like a fish out of water. I wasn't able to scream and the more I tried to pull the cat the more he cemented his progress and ripped at my flesh with his claws.

I slapped the bed beside me in a desperate attempt to find Rachel and alert her to the horrific situation. I needed her help. I had to remove the cat before he suffocated me or ripped open my esophagus. But Rachel wasn't in the bed. I wanted to think it was a nightmare. I tried to tell myself to wake up. But the pain was tremendous and nothing I'd ever experienced in a nightmare and I knew there was no mistake. This was not a dream. This wasn't a fever-induced hallucination. This wasn't a mental illness. This was real and I was going to die.

Flecks of red began to swirl in the darkness and I knew my vision was being affected from the lack of oxygen. I pulled frantically at the cat and tried to sit up. The cat had invaded far enough down my throat that I could feel his head in the center of my chest like the worst case of heart burn I'd ever experienced. It felt like I'd swallowed a cinderblock. The cat's hind legs and tail were the only parts left protruding from my mouth. I'd begun to sweat profusely and my hands kept slipping from his squirming back legs. I desperately thrashed on the bed in a last attempt to call attention to my dire situation or to squish the cat and force him to retreat.

Where was Rachel? Couldn't she hear me struggling? Didn't she know I was dying? Did she even care?

My arms and legs began to tingle and became weak. My stomach burned and swelled as the last of the cat slid down my throat and past my windpipe. I was finally able to swallow large gulps of air. But the rise and fall of my chest caused even more pain.

I began to shake uncontrollably and I tried to process what had happened and how the fuck I was still alive. *This isn't real,* I told myself.

The cat scratched my insides and fidgeted until he was able to curl up into a comfortable position like a demented fetus in its mother's belly. Rivulets of sweat poured down my body. The pain was excruciating and I thought if this was real I would lose consciousness any moment and slip into the soft dark void of death. I could taste blood and I groaned as I struggled to my feet.

I had to turn the light on. Once I turned the light on there would be something out of place or the dream would transition into something else completely illogical and the cat would disappear and I would wake up to find Rachel beside me and the damn cat asleep on my chest and I would roll over and fall back asleep and laugh it off in the morning over coffee with Rachel.

This is a dream. This is a dream. Wake up. Wake up!

I held the painful bulge in my stomach and stumbled to the light switch. The light was blinding and the pain in my gut caused me to double over. A football size and shape lump protruded from my midsection. I managed to rasp Rachel's name. I squinted against the light and saw everything with the crystal clarity of reality and knew without a doubt I wasn't dreaming.

I looked around the cabin but Rachel wasn't anywhere. The bathroom door was open and empty. Her clean clothes were still neatly folded and sitting on the dresser. The clothes of mine she'd borrowed lay discarded on the floor. Her shoes and keys still sat on the doormat by the door.

I grabbed my cellphone off the dresser and, as usual, there

was no signal. The cat shifted in my stomach. I gripped my midsection, bent over, and cried out in pain. I stumbled to the sofa and collapsed on my side, facing the coffee table. The laptop was open on the table but the screen was asleep. I touched the keypad to wake the computer. My hands were shaking violently and I was forced to wait for the computer to do its thing. I managed to sit up and opened the Internet browser. The homepage sat blank and took an extraordinarily long time to load before giving me an error code and telling me to check my Internet connection. I looked at the router box by the television and noticed none of the lights were flashing, indicating it wasn't functioning. I cursed and the cat shifted in my gut again and a twinge of red hot pain shot into the tip of my tailbone. I screamed and knew I had to get help. I assumed I was going to die anyway but I had to at least try. I had the overwhelming feeling there was nothing a doctor or hospital or even an exorcist could do for me.

If there was any hope I had one option left.

I made it to my feet and held my stomach firmly in the hopes I could keep the cat from moving and causing any more damage or pain. Time was running out. I could feel the oppressive sense of doom and death and hopelessness as I sought for one good reason why I shouldn't give up and lie down and wait for it all to end.

Rachel. Phillip. I had two reasons.

It was ridiculous to think I was in love with Rachel but there was definitely a budding of something new and wonderful and invigorating and I wanted whatever seedling we created whether it was love or obsession or just plain fucking. I needed it. And whether it continued or ended it didn't matter because at least at the end we both could say we tried and there were no regrets when you tried and failed.

And the thought of dying on Phillip was heartbreaking. I couldn't imagine how he would feel after having lost the last piece of his heritage. I know how I would feel. He was family. He had been there since the day I was born. I had known him and fought with him and loved him and looked to him for guidance and gave guidance in return for my whole life. When Dad died something of myself died with him. The same thing happened when Mom died. But I was certain anything left inside of me that could be construed as a will or a soul would be shattered the day Phillip died and I was left all alone and severed from any direct link to another human being. I thought about losing Phillip off and on since Mom's death and, when I did, an image of an astronaut drifting slowly into space without a tether to the craft they'd come from always came to mind. Phillip was the only person keeping me tethered to humanity and I hoped he felt something like that for me also and I never wanted to be the one who broke the line.

I didn't have time to dress or be bothered with any courtesies. I flung open the door and began to climb the stairs. It was raining again. But this time the raindrops were smaller and on the verge of becoming a fine mist. The water was like ice on my feverish and naked skin and sent bolts of shocking pain down my back and into my heels. I held the railing with one arm and my stomach with the other and weakly yelled for help. I began to climb the rain-slick stairs. A pain shot through my torso and I lost my footing. I banged my shin on one of the stairs and white hot pain shot up my leg. I cried out. Instead of emanating a scream a wet glob bubbled and escaped from my throat. Something broke loose in my windpipe and pooled on the back of my tongue. It had the consistency of mucus and tasted coppery. I spat it out but was unable to see it in the dark. I carefully continued up the stairs as my shin throbbed.

Once I made it to the top I noticed the faint and almost indecipherable outline of Rachel's car parked beside mine. I turned toward Lloyd's cabin. Soft orange light flickered in his windows. I strode toward his cabin as quick as the pain would allow me, limping, and ignored the gravel biting into the soles of my naked feet.

The distance between the cabins felt like it took an eternity to cross. I had to stop a few times and try to refrain from falling as the cat shifted in my gut and I was hit with a renewed wave of pain that threatened to tear me in two. Each shock of pain caused me to cry out and I expected someone in the cabin to hear me as I approached and open the door to investigate. But no shadows moved beyond the curtains to indicate anyone was even home. There was only the dance and flicker of the oil lamps from within.

The porch of the cabin was dark. I wasn't sure if there was an outside light or if they were without power. I tripped climbing the stairs and sprawled onto the wet wood. My hands hit the boards with a loud slap as I caught myself to keep from falling on my stomach. The pain I was experiencing was bad enough but I couldn't imagine what whirlwind of fury the cat would erupt into if I squished it with the weight or impact of my body hitting the ground.

Someone opened the door. I carefully lay on my side before I rolled onto my back. Tryphena stood above me, lit by the sickly yellow light spilling from the cabin door. She was naked. She bent forward to look at me and her long hair hung limply like dead tentacles reaching for my face. The light cast ghastly shadows on her face and made her appear sinister and much older. Her mouth, chin, and hands were covered in a dark shiny substance.

"Help me," I managed to rasp.

"I was starting to wonder if you were ever going to show up," she said. "Papa thought you'd be too much of a coward and would end up dying first. But I told him you fucked real good and wouldn't pass up the opportunity to bang my tight young pussy again after fucking that old hag you had earlier."

The cat stretched and acid rose in my throat. I gritted my teeth against the pain. Through clenched teeth I said, "What are you talking about?" I coughed up another glob and spat blood on the floorboards of the porch.

She placed a foot on either side of my head and squatted down over my face. She rubbed her wet cunt on my face as if she thought I was going to eat her pussy right then and there in the condition I was in. I tried to push her off but the cat's excursions through my digestive tract were weakening me with each surge of pain. She pressed her genitalia down harder on my nose and I clawed at her as I began to smother. She ignored me and moaned as if she wasn't aware I was going to die either from her vaginal suffocation or from the impossible situation of a cat crawling around in my stomach. As I struggled with Tryphena the floorboards of the cabin creaked and combined with the sound of footfalls.

Lloyd said, "Girl, get off him! He's not ready yet."

Tryphena removed her pussy from my face abruptly and stood. I gasped for air and wiped my face with the back of my arm with feeble movements. Lloyd held Tryphena by her upper arm. I would've thanked him for saving me from his crazy daughter if he wasn't also naked and sporting an erection. His mouth and hands were also covered in a dark glistening substance. It wasn't until he gave the girl a shake and let go of her arm that I recognized the stains for what they were. He had left a smeared and bloody handprint on the girl's arm. He stared at his daughter with a furious expression and began to stroke his cock as she stared down at me with the sullen look of a reprimanded child.

I thought, *I should've stayed and died in my own cabin.*

The cat's restlessness drove me from my thoughts of a peaceful death. I yelped and rolled into a fetal position.

"Please," I said. I wasn't sure if I was asking for death or help or for them to go away. Death seemed like the best option as it felt like someone had turned on a chainsaw in my stomach.

Lloyd said, "Help me get him inside." He grabbed one of my wrists.

Tryphena grabbed my other wrist and the two dragged me into the cabin. The force of the two pulling on my arms stretched my stomach tight and made the cat twist under the pressure. I didn't have the strength to scream any more. All I could do was whimper, squeeze my eyes tight against the pain, and begin to cry. They dropped me unceremoniously on the floor as hot tears slid down my face.

The floorboards creaked as they milled about. But once they were settled there was another set of footfalls resounding with a deeper thud that shook the floor as if the person was much larger than the other two.

I opened my eyes and found they had dropped me beside the kitchen table. The bottom side of the table was ill lit but I could see Tryphena sitting in the chair opposite from me. Her legs were spread and she masturbated by forming her hand into a cone and slipping her whole fist inside her cunt. She rocked her hips to hump her hand. She moaned and grunted as she fisted herself.

Lloyd passed behind her and stopped at the end of the table by my feet. There were a set of feet extended a few inches past the table top, toes up, where he stood. He stared at whoever was lying on the kitchen table, masturbated, and repeated the phrase 'oh yeah, fuck' over and over and bit his lip as he worked his cock.

Sickness coiled in the pit of my stomach as I struggled to sit up. The sensation of my fear, of the thing I feared to see on the table, ran deeper and more visceral than the damage the cat continued to inflict on me. Rage and physical pain filled me and surged through my body as I grabbed the table top and pulled myself into a sitting position.

Lloyd climbed onto the table and I was now in a position to see more than what I'd originally feared. Rachel was not just lying on the table. Rachel was naked, spread-eagle, and dead. Her head was turned in my direction and the sparkle that filled her eyes just hours ago was hazed over with the milky darkness of death. And, beyond the haze, the final moments of fear she experienced were frozen as an expression of pure terror on her face. A sorrow more enormous than anything I'd ever experienced welled up inside of me and spilled over. My eyes darted down Rachel's now grayish body and focused on the dark new opening on her stomach. They'd cut her from under her breasts to a few inches above her pubis mons and her insides were exposed and glistening under the dancing flames of the oil lamps.

I wailed like a wounded animal but the other two ignored me.

Lloyd was on the table, repositioning Rachel's lifeless legs. Once he was satisfied with her position he guided his cock inside of her pussy. He fucked her dead body fast and kept repeating 'oh yeah, fuck' while propping himself up to stare at the open wound in her stomach. Tryphena continued to masturbate while eating something pink and bloody from her free hand. Nausea surged through me and I began to retch as I fruitlessly swatted at Lloyd. Nothing was freed from my stomach but a small bit of bile and spittle which stretched from my lip to the tabletop as I tried to crawl on the table and clawed at Lloyd's wrist in a puny attempt to pull him off Rachel.

The cat scrambled and shifted as I retched again and my stomach muscles worked to help expel him from my body. My strength faltered and I collapsed back onto the floor and began convulsing. I managed to roll onto my side and was forced to witness the grotesque scene playing out at the kitchen table. I could only see Lloyd as he continued to thrust. The cat clawed its way back up my throat as my body shook uncontrollably.

The sound of Lloyd's naked flesh against Rachel's caused something essential in my mind to snap. The physical pain my body was experiencing vibrated and I went numb. The cat lodged himself in my throat and blocked my ability to breathe once again. I heaved hard causing my ears to ring and my face to fill with blood. Lloyd let out an exuberant cry as he climaxed and collapsed on top of Rachel.

The cat's slimy head worked its way up the back of my throat, into my mouth, and past my lips. Once his whole head emerged from my mouth I tried to grab him with shaky hands and pull him out so I could breathe. The only thing I managed to accomplish was to get bitten several times before relenting to allow the damn thing to escape on its own or kill me.

Lloyd climbed down from the table and took a seat at the head of the table, which happened to be at Rachel's feet. He rubbed his softening penis and panted to regain his breath.

The cat managed to pull its front legs free and placed them on my collarbone to pull himself the rest of the way out. The wet cat stood beside me and shook indignantly. I gasped for air in short bursts and cried. The cat furiously began to lick himself to clean off the blood and bile it was saturated in.

The footsteps I associated with something large approached. I was assaulted with a scent similar to clove that stung my nostrils and tickled my sinuses and urged me to sneeze. The person slid its slender and cool hands under me. A part of my brain comprehended everything happening but my body was exhausted and vibrating and sweating and I was sure I was sinking deep into shock since I was unable to feel any pain.

The person lifted me easily with sinewy arms and cradled me against their boney chest like an infant. I lifted my head to look at their face. The word 'it' replaced 'person' when I took in the face appraising me. The pupils of its large eyes were irregular and the eyes were set far apart in its elongated and misshaped head. It wasn't a person with an odd deformity. This was something else. Another species. Its skin was cool and unnatural and had a sickly hue to it. It did not have lips but a large slit for a mouth. The slit opened and tried to mimic a human smile but only managed to form a demented grimace revealing several rows of canine-like teeth. Terror soared through my already vibrating body and my heart kicked into an overdrive I thought it was already in. The image of this thing turning me into a snack the way Lloyd and Tryphena fed from Rachel filled my mind. I tried to scream but my throat was raw from the cat and all I could manage was a faint squeak. I began to fight the thing holding me but my weak flailing seemed to annoy the thing and I knew it was pointless. My muscles had reached their limit and they were comprised of the lame and spent aches of a flu a thousand times more crippling than anything I'd ever experienced. My terror and humiliation to fight back brought fresh torrents of tears from my eyes. The thing carried me to the far side of the cabin and laid me on the bed. My hoarse wailing caught in my damaged throat and caused me to cough up more blood which slid from the corner of my mouth and ran down my neck.

From the bed I could see Lloyd and Tryphena were indifferent to what was happening to me and they continued to eat pieces of Rachel. The thing loomed over me as I lay on the bed. It turned its head back and forth as if it were inspecting me or smelling me. It was unnaturally tall and lanky with long slender arms and hands. It had a pulsing slit in its stomach where a bellybutton should be. The slit opened and closed like a mouth and there was only a smooth pubis mons where genitalia should've been located. There was no sign of breasts but I knew the thing was female or as close to a female gender its kind could be. It suddenly struck me that it looked similar to the wooden effigy I'd seen in the woods.

The damp cat jumped on the bed and curled up by my head. The creature also climbed awkwardly onto the bed and positioned itself over me. It grabbed my deflated penis with its bony and probing fingers. I tried to slap its hand away and roll onto my side. It ignored me and took advantage of my feeble state. It lowered its belly toward my retracted dick and desperately tried to place my soft penis inside the cold slit on its stomach. I smacked at the creature's huge head and it reared back and hissed at me. Its breath smelled like grave dirt and it kept its inhuman eyes locked on mine as it worked. My cock would not comply as the thing's cold slit pulsed and sucked on it like a mouth, even trying to swallow my balls. The thing stared at me, not moving, as it tried to fuck me. I turned my head to the side and squeezed my eyes shut. The thing hissed in my face a final time before giving up its fruitless pursuit and leaving the bed.

The creature lifted me from the bed and was less gentle about moving me the second time. A thought crossed my mind and I wondered if it was offended I didn't find it sexually attractive. That thought and the absurdity of the situation and the exhaustion and wear and tear my body had undergone caused me to burst into hysterical laughter, which sounded more like a wet gurgle, as the thing carried me toward the table.

There was a sloshing noise and I turned my head toward it as we rounded the table. Tryphena's head bobbed up and down in Lloyd's lap. He held the back of her head and fondled his balls as she sucked his cock.

The thing propped me up in a chair across from Lloyd. An empty plate with a fork on one side and a knife on the other separated me from Rachel's head. I was forced to watch Lloyd as his daughter fellated him.

Lloyd slapped the side of Tryphena's head hard. "Get off, girl. Don't be rude to the company."

She pulled off his cock and rubbed the side of her head indignantly as she returned to her seat to the right of me. The creature took the last seat on my left in a ridiculous gesture of humanity. It looked as absurd as a giant sitting at a children's table.

Tryphena and Lloyd's plates and utensils were spattered with gore. I reached forward and took Rachel's head in my hands and turned her face toward me. Her skin was cool and clammy and I leaned forward to place my forehead against hers. I began to bawl and my emotional exertions almost caused me to fall from the chair. The creature's arms were long enough to push me back into a sitting position without leaving its chair.

As I was being pushed back my arms were forced away from Rachel's head and dragged across the table. I flailed and managed to take up the knife and fork. I slashed at the thing's arm with the knife and managed to cause a small wound. It hissed at me, grabbed my knife-wielding hand, and forced me to ram the knife deep into my own eye socket.

Several things happened at once. The creature let out a purr of pleasure, Lloyd and Tryphena erupted into cheers much like fans attending a sporting event, I dropped the fork I was holding in the other hand, and . . . I felt no pain. I could feel the knife was deep into my eye and beyond. I could feel the pressure and smooth cold metal of the blade resting above my sinuses and inside my brain. And everything went completely numb. My aching muscles ceased. The raw feeling in my throat was gone. The burning inside my stomach the cat had created was eliminated. I turned my head to the side to use my good eye to see the other three. They stared at me expectantly and I was convinced what I was experiencing and seeing were the last desperate glitches of my brain's firing synapses before I died. I remembered the old myth of the beheaded being able to see and compute for ten seconds after their head had been severed.

I became vaguely aware my hand was still clutching the handle of the blade. I wasn't sure if I should remove it or not. What if removing the blade caused more damage? What if my brain liquefied and poured out of my eye socket? I decided I didn't have anything left to lose at this point and would be better off dead. Rachel was dead and I was sure they were toying with me like a cat toying with a mouse before it devoured the weaker creature. If I wasn't about to collapse into death because of the knife I was certain I was going to experience even more atrocious tortures momentarily that would make me wish I was dead. I slowly removed the knife and realized my strength had returned. I was certain the deadening of the pain and the surge of energy were a result of an adrenaline rush. I had to take advantage of this chemically-induced superpower.

My vison was restored in my eye once the blade was fully

removed but the picture the eye formed was distorted and blurry. The bad vision in one and clear in the other was disorienting and gave me vertigo.

Tryphena watched me with a delighted expression and rage flooded my body. Her gore-covered mouth was a reminder she had most likely played a role in Rachel's death. I closed my bad eye to regain my equilibrium and leapt out of my chair and pounced on Tryphena. Her chair toppled when I collided with her and we both tumbled to the floor. I straddled her and lifted the knife high above my head. She scratched at my chest and screamed and kicked like a wild animal. I tried to growl but somehow I knew whatever the cat had done to my throat would never be repaired and the best I would ever manage would be grunts of pleasure or discourse. I plunged the knife deep into Tryphena's breast where I assumed her blackened heart would be if she even possessed one.

"Fuck!" Tryphena yelled.

I opened my bad eye and watched in amazement as her struggles only increased. In my distorted peripheral I spotted Lloyd getting to his feet and knocking his chair backward in the process.

"Damn it, boy!" he shouted. "You best come to your senses!"

He rounded the table to approach us. Tryphena squirmed beneath me. There was a large crash as the table was upended behind me. Rachel's body rolled onto me and her weight caused me to collapse onto Tryphena. The handle of the knife protruding from Tryphena's chest bit between my ribs. I cried out but only managed to honk like a goose. The air was filled with the graveyard scent of the creature's breath as it hissed its displeasure.

"Get off me!" Tryphena yelled in my ear.

The weight of Rachel was suddenly gone and the creature wrenched me off Tryphena by my arm and tossed me backward. I landed hard on my tailbone and scuttled backward until my back hit a wall. Lloyd righted the table into its original position. The thing lifted Rachel's body haphazardly and spilled her intestines on the ground before dumping her on the table. Lloyd picked up the chairs and set them in their previous positions with a hard slap on the wooden floor. The thing scooped up Rachel's innards and set them back in the open cavity in her stomach.

I sprung to my feet and bolted for the door. But the thing was quick and grabbed me by the neck. It forced me to sit in the same chair. It held me one handed by the neck in a vice-like grip, its long fingers wrapping completely around my neck in a relentless collar.

Tryphena took her original chair also. The knife still protruded from her chest and her hair was a tousled mess. She appeared aggravated and flabbergasted when she looked down at the knife. She grabbed the handle and yanked it free. A small trickle of blood escaped the wound and she slapped the knife on the table. Lloyd stood beside her, assessing her wound.

"Idiot," she growled. "You can't die once you feed it. You don't know anything." She turned to her father. "I told you—!"

He slapped her face. "Don't sass me!"

She rubbed her cheek with an umbrageous expression. The creature still held me by the neck but turned its attention to the other two. I wanted to ask Tryphena to elaborate but even if the creature hadn't been been gripping my throat too tight I wouldn't be able to speak. The cat hopped up on the table and appraised me nonchalantly for a brief moment before approaching Rachel's open stomach and tentatively begin chewing on a piece of her intestines.

I moaned and wanted to close my eyes and block it all out but Lloyd abruptly left the table and went into the kitchen area and began rummaging around in a drawer. The creature returned its attention to me. Lloyd produced a meat cleaver from the drawer and returned to the table.

Tryphena stood and held out her hand to him. "Let me do it."

"Don't go mutilatin' her face like a jealous hog," he said. "I want a couple more good fucks first." He handed her the cleaver with a hard and reprimanding glare and began to stroke his semi-hardened cock.

She sighed. "One time! You're never going to let me hear the end of it."

Tryphena grabbed Rachel's right hand. She bent her arm in an unnatural way. I clutched the creature's hand and bucked but it only squeezed my neck harder.

I could feel the blood in my face swelling and a glob of something leaked from my wounded eye and slid down my cheek. Tryphena lifted the cleaver and brought it down hard and fast. She severed Rachel's double thumb. She picked up the knife that had been buried in my eye and her chest and began to fillet the flesh from the bone.

Once she was done she picked up a large chunk of the tissue she'd harvested and approached me. She dangled the meat in front of my face and said, "Is this what you want? Huh? This is it, right? You wanted to fuck her because she was a freak!"

I tried to shake my head and put some distance between me and the bit of Rachel she was shoving in my face. Lloyd leered at me as he slowly and purposefully climbed onto the table with a fully erect cock and shooed the cat away from Rachel's open stomach. I bucked and beat at the creature's hand but it was like fighting a cement statue.

Tryphena savagely ripped the flesh she held into two pieces. The meat made a sucking sound when it gave. Lloyd guided his cock inside of Rachel's cunt and began fucking her and chewing on one of her nipples like a dog chewing on a rawhide toy. I let loose a sound that could only be considered half human and half garbled.

Tryphena took one of the halves of Rachel she held and began to insert it into the slit on the creature's stomach. The opening wrapped around her fingers and nursed on them like an infant suckling a tit. The thing purred as its stomach opening made wet noises and eventually released the girl's fingers sans the tidbit of meat.

Lloyd wrenched Rachel's nipple free from her body with a sound like material ripping. He chewed it open-mouthed like it was bubble gum and pulled his cock out of Rachel's corpse and sat on his haunches. He scooped up a handful of Rachel's offal from the wound and began to masturbate with it while staring down at her and saying 'oh yeah, fuck' over and over while biting his lip.

The girl turned her attention to me. "Communion time," she said.

She tried to shove the piece of meat into my mouth. I clenched my jaw and pressed my lips tight. Her fingers managed to probe past my lips and she rubbed the flesh on my teeth and gums. She grew agitated with my resistance and scratched my gums with her fingernails. I tried to shake my head away from her.

She yelled, "Come on! This is it! It's almost over! Eat it! Fucking eat it!" She pulled the meat out of my cheek and changed strategies. She straddled my lap and ground her cunt against my soft penis. She pressed her breasts against my chest and kissed me. She tried to press her tongue between my lips but only succeeded in sloppily licking my face. She sat back and in a sweet voice said, "Come on, baby. You'll be able to fuck me from now till eternity. We'll never grow old. My pussy will be pink and young forever. Come on. You've had a taste. You liked it. Don't you like the way my pussy tastes? Will my pussy juice help the medicine go down?" She reached between her legs and inserted the piece of flesh inside her vagina. She worked it in and out a couple of times, smiling at me, before trying to force it into my mouth again.

I sucked in my lips this time and bit down on them hard enough to draw blood. I hoped it would keep her from rubbing the piece on my gums and teeth again. She gave up quickly this time and looked to the creature, flabbergasted. The thing looked back and forth between the two of us before lifting its free hand and forcing four of its fingers into my mouth. I tried to bite its fingers and only managed to bite my lower lip harder as it grabbed my lower jaw and jerked it downward until something in my jaw popped loudly by my ear. A throb of pain shot into my ear and down my neck. I let out a strangled cry. Blood filled my mouth and I coughed, spraying the two. The creature let go of my throat. I bucked wildly and threw Tryphena to the floor but the creature held steadfast to my lower jaw, which now seemed only to be attached to one side of my face. The skin stretched and burned on one side of my face as the creature pulled on my jaw. I was vaguely aware of the sex sounds coming from Lloyd's direction as I struggled to keep from drowning or having my lower jaw completely ripped off. The creature shoved its fingers from its other hand in my mouth and grabbed the upper part of my head to pry open my mouth and hold it that way. I pounded on the thing's hard and unmoving arms and kicked at it and continued to gag and choke on the blood, spraying it on myself and the creature. In the peripheral of my good eye I noticed Tryphena had made it to her feet. She approached me with the piece of Rachel's flesh again. I kicked at her before she lunged at me and rammed her hand in my mouth and probed the back of my tongue with her fingers. Her fingers caused me to dry heave and, as much as it terrified me and I struggled for it not to happen, Rachel's flesh hit a point of no return and slid down my throat. I desperately tried to cough it back up but there was no hope.

The world spun and darkened and I became lightheaded. I began to spin head over heels at a blinding rate as the world became darker and darker around the edges until there was nothing left except for Tryphena's triumphant cry and Lloyd yelling he was coming. It all left me. And the world became nothing. And I was left with the strong scent of clove and the taste of blood.

22

The sour scent of the wounds and my unclean mouth assaulted my nostrils as I sat in the shadows inside the back of the cabin. I sat in a chair opposite the front door and stared through the screen door and down the drive at Phillip's car. He'd parked beside my car . . . where Rachel's car had been. Lloyd had left to run errands hours ago and I wasn't sure what running errands all entailed for these three but I could only imagine.

I pinched the end of the straw protruding from the bottle filled with what Lloyd and Tryphena jokingly called my 'meal replacement'. I carefully pressed the straw between my lips and sucked the pureed matter into my mouth. I fought the urge to gag against the gamey taste of my new diet. A small piece of tissue that wasn't pureed well caught in the back of my throat. I cleared my throat to try and dislodge the thing.

Tryphena stood in the doorway and watched for Phillip. The thing sat in a chair behind the door and both of them looked at me when I cleared my throat as if the noise I'd made was me trying to convey a message to either one of them. When I made no further attempt to communicate with them they ignored me.

I took another tentative sip. Swallowing was hell. Half of the discomfort was from my raw throat. The other half came when I tried to swallow and the movement of my throat fought against the material wrapped under my jaw and tied at the top of my head. I wasn't sure how long it would take for my jaw to heal or how long I needed to look like Jacob Marley's ghost. I didn't really care anymore. Nothing mattered anymore. Time didn't matter. Money didn't matter. Even . . .

Phillip reappeared at the top of the stairs. I closed my healed and permanently discolored eye and focused with my other to watch him. He walked over to my car and tried the door handle. I never kept my doors locked since moving here. He disappeared into my car.

I sucked in the last bit of the puree. My straw made the empty rattling noise on the bottom of the bottle and Tryphena shushed me. The puree was going rotten with no electricity to refrigerate it. I was assuming it was one of the many reasons Lloyd was gone.

Phillip stepped into the middle of the drive and looked around as if he were lost. He looked to our cabin and Tryphena stepped back from the door and into the darkness of the shadows. Phillip slowly walked toward our cabin with his hands on his hips, staring at the ground. He climbed the steps to the door and craned his head to look inside. He squinted and I knew he could only see what I saw when I'd done the exact same thing. Nothing but darkness.

He knocked on the frame of the screen door and called, "Hello?"

Tryphena approached the door and said, "Can I help you?"

"Oh. I didn't think anyone was here. Hey, you wouldn't have happened to see my brother around, have you?"

"Today?"

"Well, yeah, today."

"His car is there." She pointed at my car.

"But have you actually seen him? Walking around outside."

"Uh . . . Nope."

"Have you seen him in the last couple of days?"

Tryphena mimed thoughtful contemplation. "I don't think so."

Worry lines creased Phillip's face and there was a slight tremble in his voice whenever he was anxious. At least when you're dead you don't have to see the anguish your loved ones have to endure when you're gone. This was worse than any punishment I might receive if there was an afterlife. Having the last living person who meant anything to me mere feet away and wanting to call out to him and tell him I was here but knowing it would be better if he thought I was dead was awful. I pressed the heel of my palm into my good eye and tried to stave off the racking sobs I could feel behind a thin veil of what was left of my humanity. I slid my hand into my pocket and ran my thumb over the smooth braided lock of Rachel's hair I now kept to calm me.

The air shifted in the cabin and one of the floorboards squeaked near me. I lifted my head to find the creature standing over me. The opening in its stomach gaped in a beckoning manner and I complied. I stuck two fingers in the slit and it closed on them and suckled and fed on my misery and suffering and tried to comfort me. Euphoria slowly washed over me and replaced my despair and Typhena and Phillip's banter was no longer important. Their conversation became background noise as the creature nursed. When I was empty and no longer felt anything the creature left me to hide in the shadows behind the door again.

When I came to my senses Tryphena was standing on the porch smoking a cigarette and Phillip's car was rounding the turn to climb the driveway. I knew these last brief seconds would be the last time I ever saw him. I stood and crossed the cabin and stood in the doorframe as Phillip's taillights disappeared behind the line of trees. I pressed my forehead against the screen.

Tryphena spoke without turning to acknowledge me. "He's going to report you missing and the police are going to come." She took a pull from her smoke and exhaled slowly before speaking again. "Hasn't heard from you since you went hiking with a girl named Rachel."

The creature walked up behind me and purred softly. Tryphena took a pull from her smoke and exhaled slowly. I pushed the screen door open and stepped outside.

She said, "I don't think you should be outside. You never know who'll be coming down the drive now. We need to pack before Papa gets home." She crushed her cigarette.

I ignored her and stared down the driveway. The cat emerged from the tree line and trotted toward the porch and meowed for food. Tryphena pestered me again to go back inside but I blocked her out. She eventually scooped up the cat and retreated back into the cabin.

I stood on the porch, waiting. I wasn't sure how much time passed. A lot of banging of the dresser's drawers and kitchen cabinets came from the cabin and Tryphena periodically scolded me and demanded I come inside and threatened me with punishments worse than the death that would never take me into the quiet bliss of nothingness and release me from a never-ending hell on earth. I continued to stand in the same spot, unmoving, as the afternoon gave way to evening and the sun began to set. I waited as the insects began their evening song and the birds returned to their nests for the night. And I wished I'd been born some small dumb animal who would've lived a short life of eating and fucking and reproducing and getting eaten by a larger animal or hit by a car.

Tryphena cursed within the cabin, either speaking to herself or the creature about my insolence. The sun was nearly set and the day was coming to an end when a flash of light within the trees along the slope of the drive caught my attention. The unmistakable and faint sound of crunching gravel beneath car tires announced someone was coming.

C.V. Hunt is the author of several unpopular books.

www.authorcvhunt.com

Other Grindhouse Press Titles

#666__*Satanic Summer* by Andersen Prunty

#032__*This Town Needs A Monster* by Andersen Prunty

#031__*The Fetishists* by A.S. Coomer

#030__*Ritualistic Human Sacrifice* by C.V. Hunt

#029__*The Atrocity Vendor* by Nick Cato

#028__*Burn Down the House and Everyone In It* by Zachary T. Owen

#027__*Misery and Death and Everything Depressing* by C.V. Hunt

#026__*Naked Friends* by Justin Grimbol

#025__*Ghost Chant* by Gina Ranalli

#024__*Hearers of the Constant Hum* by William Pauley III

#023__*Hell's Waiting Room* by C.V. Hunt

#022__*Creep House: Horror Stories* by Andersen Prunty

#021__*Other People's Shit* by C.V. Hunt

#020__*The Party Lords* by Justin Grimbol

#019__*Sociopaths In Love* by Andersen Prunty

#018__*The Last Porno Theater* by Nick Cato

#017__*Zombieville* by C.V. Hunt

#016__*Samurai Vs. Robo-Dick* by Steve Lowe

#015__*The Warm Glow of Happy Homes* by Andersen Prunty

#014__*How To Kill Yourself* by C.V. Hunt

#013__*Bury the Children in the Yard: Horror Stories* by Andersen Prunty

#012 __*Return to Devil Town (Vampires in Devil Town Book Three)* by Wayne Hixon

#011__*Pray You Die Alone: Horror Stories* by Andersen Prunty

#010__*King of the Perverts* by Steve Lowe

#009__*Sunruined: Horror Stories* by Andersen Prunty

#008__*Bright Black Moon (Vampires in Devil Town Book Two)* by Wayne Hixon

#007__*Hi I'm a Social Disease: Horror Stories* by Andersen Prunty

#006__*A Life On Fire* by Chris Bowsman

#005__*The Sorrow King* by Andersen Prunty

#004__*The Brothers Crunk* by William Pauley III

#003__*The Horribles* by Nathaniel Lambert

#002__*Vampires in Devil Town* by Wayne Hixon

#001__*House of Fallen Trees* by Gina Ranalli

#000__*Morning is Dead* by Andersen Prunty

Made in the USA
Lexington, KY
04 July 2019